CATCH RIDER

JENNIFER H. LYNE

Houghton Mifflin Harcourt | Boston New York

Quotations on pp. 35, 117–19, and 222–23 are from George H. Morris, *Hunter Seat Equitation* (New York: Doubleday, 1990).

www.hmhbooks.com

The text was set in Adobe Jenson Pro.

The Library of Congress has cataloged the hardcover edition as follows:
Lyne, Jennifer H.
Catch rider/by Jennifer H. Lyne.
p. cm.
Summary: Despite her poor background and ferocious competition from more privileged girls, fourteen-year-old Sid pursues her dream of becoming a catch rider—a show rider who can ride anything—with help from her Uncle Wayne.
[1. Horsemanship—Fiction. 2. Horse shows—Fiction. 3. Uncles—Fiction.
4. Social classes—Fiction. 5. Single-parent families—Fiction.
6. Family life—Virginia—Fiction. 7. Virginia—Fiction.] I. Title.
PZ7.L98498Cat 2013
[Fic]—dc23 201202261

ISBN: 978-0-547-86871-4 hardcover
ISBN: 978-0-544-30182-5 paperback

Manufactured in the United States
DOC 10 9 8 7 6 5 4 3 2 1
4500457713

To my family

For my boys

After the Round © 1988 by Ann Lyne

Lonely people have enthusiasms which cannot always be explained. . . . When something touches their emotions, it runs through them like Paul Revere, awakening feelings that gather into great armies.

—Mark Helprin, *Winter's Tale*

ONE

IT WAS RAINING hard and the lightning was getting close. I ran the red gelding down the path in Dunn's Gap and listened for that moment when a horse is at a full gallop and none of his feet touch the ground, because during that split second, we're flying. I pretended we were racing a train as the trees whizzed by, their branches scraping my jacket. I lay down on the horse's neck to avoid a low branch. Water dripped off my riding hat into my mouth, tasting of sweaty nylon. I spat it out and wiped my face on my sleeve while I kept my eyes up, banking around a muddy turn.

As we galloped, the rain came down in a roar. I was soaked through. The reins were slippery and I fought to keep a grip on the horse. I dug my fingers into his dirty mane and around his martingale strap to hang on. I'd tied his tail into a tight mud-knot, wrapping it around itself into a ball so it didn't fall past his hocks. It would be easier to get the mud out later.

The red horse took the bit in his mouth, bore down, and

ran for it like he was loose in the field. He must have forgotten I was there. His ears were forward and he wanted to go, but it was slick, and running like this in the mud was dangerous. If he stumbled, he could send us both down the ravine. One shoe clinked loudly against an old rusted pipe that was gushing rainwater down into the creek below, but it didn't interrupt his stride or worry him one bit. I listened to the confident, rhythmic hoofbeats, and I grinned.

Quick thoughts began to flicker in and out of my mind. This was the last of the big summer storms and the last day before school started. Every time I thought about it, I felt sick to my stomach. I hated school. I couldn't sit in a plastic desk all day, couldn't stand being inside under those awful lights with those teachers staring down at me. If you had to squeeze yourself into a girdle to stand up and try to teach a bunch of hillbilly kids — well, that was just pathetic. I hated the way it smelled at school, the way the rednecks in the hallway would yell and scream like they owned the place.

One time I'd heard a boy say, "That's Jimmy Criser's girl — they live in that shitty little gray house behind Hardee's." When another boy laughed, I looked at him and said, "Well, at least my daddy ain't a drunk like yours." We all know things about each other in Covington. And people who make fun of me wish they hadn't.

All these kids thought they were cool, but I knew they'd

never amount to a damn thing. They'd work in the paper mill until the day they died. I know that sounds mean and angry, but I'm not either one. We have a life to live that could stop any minute, and I guess I can't believe this is how some people want to spend it. It makes me sad as hell. I want to ask them, don't they want to know what's out there? I sure do.

One day, I'd win the Bath County Horse Show up in Hot Springs, where all the rich kids competed every June. I'd jump every fence perfectly on a big, shiny, braided hunter, and I'd jog my horse into the ring to claim the silver cup and tricolor championship ribbon. The wealthy kids lining the rail would say, "Damn, that girl can ride anything." Melinda, my mother, would stop cursing horses and love them like she used to, and her dirtbag of a boyfriend would fear me. The kids at school would whisper to each other, "How'd she learn to ride like that?" And some kid might say, "She's the best rider I ever saw."

I stood up in the stirrups and planted my hands on the red horse's withers to slow him down. He pulled against me, and I wondered if I'd have to run him into the bank to make him stop. I couldn't hear Wayne's horse at all. The creek always ran hard and loud back there behind Coles Mountain. It probably sounded just like this two or three hundred years ago. I wished for an instant that I could have lived back then and spent my days running through the woods on a horse. If you were fourteen in those days, Jimmy used to tell me, you worked just like the adults, didn't waste your time at school. Kids were baling hay with a team of horses at nine years old.

The red horse tore around a turn, his ears shot up, and he slammed to a stop. My feet came out of the stirrups, and I had to tighten my knees like a vise to hang on. What the heck had he seen? Maybe June, hiding behind a tree?

The horse snorted hard, and finally I saw what he saw: a hickory had fallen across the path, gotten caught in another tree. Damn, he had good eyes. I could barely see it. Some horses can stand right next to a locomotive and not mind one bit, but others will damn near tear the barn down if a woodchuck runs by. I was right. This red horse didn't shy at anything. His eyes were locked right on that fallen tree in a way that made my palms sweat.

I waited a moment for Uncle Wayne to catch up. I heard the smack of another horse's hooves, and my uncle galloped out of the fog on his brown horse and stopped too. His horse was blowing hard with his chest lathered up. Uncle Wayne squinted, his face slick from the rain running off his baseball cap. He cursed. It would take forever for us to backtrack, and the hill was too steep to walk the horses around the fallen tree. They'd be up to their hocks in mud, and I imagined us sliding down the hill, a tangle of reins and hooves, into the ravine. Horse people are always walking that line between being brave and being crazy. Sometimes it just depends on how things end up.

The red horse looked at the fallen tree and pulled on the reins, wanting to go. It must have been four feet high, and I had never jumped anything that big. The horse faced the jump and squared himself up for it.

"Hell no!" yelled Uncle Wayne.

I felt the horse coiled like a spring underneath me, and I dug my heels into his sides. He planted his hind feet in the mud, got his hindquarters up under himself, and took three big strides. But he got in too close. He sprang out of the mud and must have cleared that fallen tree by a foot. I tried to hang on, but even though I had a handful of mane, I was left behind. When he landed, he shook me loose. I fell hard in the mud, and everything stopped.

I heard Uncle Wayne's voice calling, "Sid!"

Still holding the reins, I put my hands to my face, opened my eyes, and realized the horse was gone. The bridle lay next to me — I guess I'd pulled it right off his head. Now he was running around Dunn's Gap wearing nothing but a saddle in the pouring rain.

Wayne was on foot in the woods twenty feet away, trying to get to me. He swore again as he helped the brown horse pick his way through the rocks and briars. Finally they made it through, and I looked up at Wayne's face in the rain. I could see the outline of his skull in his tan skin, and his blue eyes sparkled like big aquamarines. Maybe he was the Grim Reaper, coming to take me to heaven.

"What's the West Virginia state flower?" he asked me.

"The satellite dish," I said.

I felt for my teeth to make sure they were all there.

"Damn it, girl!" he shouted. "You're lucky you didn't kill yourself!"

I sat up, dizzy and confused, my riding hat lying in the wet weeds. When I inhaled, pain shot out from my ribs. I had a metallic taste in my mouth from the shock. I felt like my bones had crashed into each other.

"When you ride my horse, you damn well do what I tell you," he said.

I was ashamed.

"I just found that red horse in an auction pen last Thursday," he continued. "I don't know a thing about him —"

"He can jump," I interrupted.

"Well, that's good, ain't it?" Wayne said sharply, looking me in the eye. He was scaring me. Sometimes he looked exactly like Melinda. His little sister, my mother.

He put his hands on his knees and stood up.

"We better go find that half-nekked horse 'fore somebody calls the sheriff," he said.

We walked together down the path, the wet brown horse hanging his head. I slipped a little in the mud, and Wayne grabbed my elbow. "Watch yourself. Slick as a fat baby's ass out here."

We found the red horse by the side of the road looking embarrassed, with one stirrup caught on a farmer's mailbox.

TWO

I HAVE RED HAIR and green eyes, but I'm not Irish. My ancestors were from England and came over here in the 1600s. One of them, Colonel Criser, fought in the Revolutionary War. He was surrounded by the British, but he fought them off with his men and made their supplies last long enough to get out. He was in some kind of trouble at one point for saying bad things about the minutemen, but nobody knows what he said. That's just like a Criser, getting mad and shooting off his mouth.

Even though my family has been here since the very first boat from England, before the *Mayflower*, it doesn't mean we were rich and had a whole bunch of slaves fanning us on the porch. I'm sure my ancestors were as poor as dirt. I hope they didn't have slaves, or if they did, I hope they were nice to them. If I came into this world and realized my family had a bunch of slaves, I'd be really nice to them. It always cracks me up when kids at school get mad about illegal Mexicans coming up here. I want to say, *Good thing my grandfather didn't feel that way about yours or he'd have sent him packing.* Nobody could send *me* packing but an American Indian.

It took us a full hour to get back to the barn at Wayne's place. We untacked the horses in the run-in shed while the rain leaked through the roof and made big puddles in the sawdust.

"Get that tack dried off. Hang the saddle pads up, and put some Absorbine on his legs after running him like that," Wayne said. Grumpy as usual. Every time I finished one thing, he gave me a list of ten more.

I pulled the dirty orange bottle of Absorbine off the shelf, cupped my hand, poured the green liquid into it, and held it against the ligaments under the horse's knee. The horse blinked and looked around at his new home. I always felt sorry for a new horse — just showing up in some new barn, no friends, no idea of how he was going to be treated. Horses weren't like stray cats or dogs, who could escape and live by their wits. They were property.

I figured this horse knew right away I was a good rider, but that didn't mean much. He could easily have been sold to a cuss of a man who beat him with a stick or to a lady who kept him in a bed of pine shavings for the rest of his life. That used to make my heart ache, but not anymore. I knew if you wanted to be a good horseman, you'd better remember they ain't pets. As Jimmy and Wayne had told me many times, *Whatever you do, don't marry your horse.*

When I was about eight, I saw Wayne smack a horse in the head for rearing up and striking at him with his front feet. I yelled at him to stop, and he said, "Damn it, girl, that horse could kill you. You think real hard before you feel sorry for him." He and Jimmy were rough when they had to be, so horses didn't cross them.

Now Wayne took good care of his horses because they'd be more valuable that way, not because they were his pets. I think Wayne did things when he was younger that he wasn't proud of now, such as shooting up a horse with a little painkiller before a show or poling — teaching a young horse to jump by raising the pole up while he's in midair, making him hit his hooves. These things are illegal now. But horses knew not to mess with him or he'd lay them right out.

The Absorbine soaked into the horse's skin. I cupped my hand again, poured more, and rubbed it onto my lower back, feeling the icy shock and smelling the menthol.

Wayne picked up a fifty-pound sack of feed from where the Southern States delivery man had stacked them beneath the overhang. He slung it over his shoulder. I did the same, breathing out so I could hoist it up, feeling the pain in my ribs. I looked at the veins in my skinny forearms and wished they'd pop out of the muscle like Uncle Wayne's did. I could be a weightlifter, my arms would still look like a couple of broomsticks.

I ripped a bag open and poured the feed into an empty barrel, then picked out a small black chunk of molasses caked with raw oats and put it in my mouth. It was sweet but dry, and I chewed, pretending I was a pony. I covered the feed barrel and locked it. The gray Shetland would eat himself to death if he got in there. I'd seen ponies who couldn't stop eating when they got their faces in a sack of sweet feed, and they'd keel over right there in the feed room. Many times I had helped a vet run a tube down a pony's nose into the belly and pump it full of mineral oil. Sometimes it worked, sometimes it didn't. I'd be happy if I never saw that again. A horse rolling in the straw groaning with colic was a horseman's worst nightmare. By that time, he'd usually twisted a gut and there was nothing left to do.

"Get that donkey some hay."

Wayne had a no-good donkey that stood out in the field and ignored everyone. He'd had him about a month.

"What's his name?"

"That donkey don't have a name."

"You got a name for him. You had him a month."

"I just call him Donkey."

"Come on."

"Mr. Wilcox."

I laughed at him. "Who's that?"

"I don't know. Just a name," he said.

Submarine stood in my way, chewing on a flake of fescue.

He was an old skewbald pinto, huge feet and knees, a little swaybacked, large head and a big belly. He had strong hooves and a powerful build. Jimmy bought him for himself on a lark when they were doing work for a fellow over in Pig Run. Uncle Wayne said Sub was the soundest horse he'd ever seen. Although most horses threw a shoe at about six weeks, Sub kept his shoes on so long, the blacksmith had to pry them off at twelve weeks. Now he just stood there chomping on the hay. He was past his prime and was a sad sight, with his long whiskers and manure stains on his white spots. He wasn't doing nothing but taking up space. He was always in the way, and it made me angry.

I shoved Sub's hindquarters over and cut my eyes at the red horse. "How much you think you can get for him?"

Wayne sized up the horse, shifting his toothpick from one cheek into the other and back. The horse had some old splints in his front legs, but they didn't seem to bother him.

"He's a short-coupled firecracker," I said. Short-backed horses tend to be hotheaded, for some reason. "Looks like one of the old-time Thoroughbreds with Arab blood, not these brittle ones you see on TV."

Wayne smirked at me, probably for repeating things I'd read in books. But he knew I was right. He leaned against the wall, crossed one leg over the other, and thought.

"He pulls on your hands," I said, still trying. I wanted

Wayne to like the horse as much as I did. "But his mouth ain't hard—he just wants to go. He's an athlete. We might try a different bit to slow him down."

Wayne felt the horse's legs for swelling, found nothing. "You know we ride everything in a D-ring. Good hands are good hands."

He grabbed a rag off a shelf and wiped mud out of the horse's nose. The horse pinned his ears back, annoyed.

"You didn't want to slow that durned horse down anyway," he said.

I wished just once I could use a different bit, a twisted-wire or a copper-mouthed snaffle, even a double-reined pelham like the ladies used when they rode sidesaddle in the old days. I imagined myself riding a jumper in a Grand Prix class at a horse show, holding his twelve hundred pounds of fury back in a fancy three-ring elevator bit.

Wayne had a strong opinion that any good rider could ride a horse in a simple bit, no tricks or shortcuts. "Fancy bits are for bad riders," he always said.

I got impatient. "So how much?"

He sucked on his dentures, pulling his cheeks down from his eye sockets until he looked like a crazy man. He snapped the teeth back in place. "A few thousand."

"That's it?"

"Been on the track so long, he can't go clockwise," he said.

I felt frustration tighten my throat. "We could fix that in the ring."

"Then fix it. I'll give you twenty percent," he said.

I knew that Uncle Wayne and his half-crooked horse-trader friends made all kinds of deals in the run-in shed with rain leaking down on them, and I wanted to make those deals too. He must have bought and sold thousands of horses — pleasure horses, carriage teams, mules, trick horses, you name it — to and from men with names like Boojie Dowdie, Apple Woodzell, or just "the Liptrap boy with the red truck." They didn't trust each other, none of them. If you were buying a horse, you had to look out for yourself — feel the horse's legs, trot him out, and ride him. If you were dumb enough to buy a lame horse or an old horse, you deserved what you got. Except sometimes Wayne would take a horse back from a good customer for credit. No money back, but he'd find him something else. Even so, I was the only person alive who really trusted him, and he was the only person I could trust.

I had read about the fancy show-horse world. It worked differently there. When a horse was for sale, the buyer's vet took x-rays and provided a report. Wayne and his fellow horse traders laughed at that. X-rays! You could tell a horse had incurable navicular disease — which Wayne called "vehicular disease" — if he tiptoed. What kind of real horseman needed a damn x-ray of a horse's legs?

I scratched the red horse's neck and he closed his eyes.
My nails left a mark as they pulled up the grit.

"You wash your horses or what?" I teased Uncle Wayne.

He flicked his toothpick into the mud.

THREE

It stopped raining, and the wind began to blow. Uncle Wayne and I walked through the sloppy paddock up to his old saltbox farmhouse. The roof was rusting at the seams and the porch hung off. We went up to Wayne's kitchen door, where Grittlebones, an old yellow cat, was sitting on the top step. He was missing teeth and his ears looked like he'd been chewed on by a pack of hyenas. He saw Wayne coming and ran under the porch.

"He looks skinny," I said.

"Then I reckon he better get to work," Wayne said.

Bouncing my left foot off the cinder block he used as a bottom step, I opened the door and went inside.

I smelled the smoke from the pine logs and the salty deer stew that had been sitting on the wood stove all day. Wayne was the only person I knew who cooked on a stove all summer. I hung my chaps over a chair by the fire to dry and got two bowls from the cupboard. As I put the stew into the bowls, Wayne opened the tin oven on top of the wood stove, pulled out a couple of biscuits wrapped in tinfoil, and handed one to me.

We sat in chairs facing each other and ate quietly. Wayne rested his heels on the wood stove, careful not to burn the rubber soles. It was only four thirty, but Wayne was usually in bed before dark.

In the old days, my mother had told me, Wayne had run around until all hours of the night. When I was growing up, he seemed to have a lady friend now and then, but it never lasted. Either she couldn't ride, she was too stupid, or she had a husband. Sometimes all three. I never liked any of them except old Beezie Winants, who was a legendary horse trader in her own right. She was the only one worth a damn. I think Beezie caught him with someone else, which was too bad, because she was a load of fun. She took me riding all the time at her place and gave me a bunch of free lessons.

The others were too flirty and pretended like he was some kind of cowboy. When I would show up to ride and see some lady hanging on the fence rail talking to him, I would find something else to do until she was gone.

Uncle Wayne worked as a farm caretaker, but he used to get a new job with a new truck every couple of years. If I asked him, he just said the old job didn't suit him, but it was really because he'd go on a crazy drunk and disappear for weeks. Then he'd sober up for another six months, or a year, or two years. My mother, Melinda, said there was no rhyme or reason to when it happened. He'd do it if things were good, and he'd do it when things were bad. Jimmy said one time that Wayne did it when he needed to get something bad out of his system, like a wave tossing a piece of garbage up on the beach. I've never been to the beach, but that's what I imagine. What it actually was — well, that was Wayne's secret.

I figured he must have stayed at this caretaker job just because the farmer there left him alone. Wayne watched the cattle and patrolled for coyotes with a rifle twice a week, and in return, he could buy and sell as many horses as he liked and keep them there.

When we finished eating, Wayne drove me home in his blue pickup. I loved that big old truck. We sat on Navajo saddle blankets. They were half polyester, not wool or anything, but they were soft. That old Ford truck had the biggest cab — felt like a tractor-trailer in there. The window handle was so big, sometimes I'd pretend I was cranking the winch on a big ship out in the ocean, raising the mainsail or whatever it's called, when I put my window up.

The mist hung over the hay fields and the water splashed into the wheel wells when we went through puddles. We passed a pond on a cattle farm, and I saw the snapping turtles poking their heads out of the warm layer of rainwater.

Whenever we passed that stretch of Route 687, I'd look out to the west and remember the time Jimmy said that the

Appalachian Mountains were the oldest in the world. Five hundred million years ago, they were the tallest mountains on earth, like the Himalayas are now. Another time he told me he'd heard that the mountains in southern China are similar, with the same trees, same climate. I figured one day I might just go there and see if this was true. Maybe I would ride one of those tough Mongolian horses on the Great Wall itself.

I looked at the creases in Wayne's face. His thick hands rested on the steering wheel, yellow stains on his fingers from smoking. Jimmy and Wayne used to stay out late and come home laughing loudly, and when I'd wake up, Wayne would be snoring on the couch. I loved those mornings. Melinda didn't like the drinking, but she and I loved all of us waking up together. We'd eat sausage and gravy, and waffles with syrup, and we'd watch cartoons. Jimmy used to laugh so hard at Daffy Duck that he could barely breathe, at how Daffy was always mad at everyone about everything. Strange how people laugh at different things. Jimmy didn't get mad about nothing.

When Jimmy died, four years ago, Melinda and Wayne pretty much stopped talking about him. They certainly didn't talk about how he died. I didn't want it this way. I guess it was the only way they could handle it. But after that I was so scared something would happen to one of them, I barely let them out of my sight without having a nervous fit. The one thing they told me about the accident was that he hit a tree on Route 220, like lots of other people had. They said it was foggy. I knew where it was, because I saw the fresh marks in the tree, but I never said anything. We'd drive right by and not say a word.

I was so scared they were going to die too and leave me that Wayne started taking me everywhere: horse auctions, farmers' co-ops, truck-stop breakfast meetings. At first, he wasn't sure what to do with me, but I didn't care. At gas stations, he'd lock the truck doors and go inside the diner to get me a hot chocolate, but I'd climb out and follow him. I tried to work up the courage to ask him if I could come live with him, but I couldn't do it. Then one day, I blurted it out while we were waiting for a train to pass at the crossing. He paused for a second, and then he said I had to live with my mother. I was embarrassed for asking and angry at him for saying no, and my face got hot. I didn't speak to him for the rest of the day, and for the first and last time, he got me a candy bar before he dropped me off.

Now we drove by Natural Well, too small to be a town, really just a dark, cold crevice in the rock that forms the well under the trees across from an old white farmhouse. When I was about six, Jimmy and I packed a lunch and went there for a picnic. I remember dropping a pebble down the well and feeling the rush of cold air on my face.

This area by the Jackson River, below the Kincaid Gorge

and running all the way up to the Richardson Gorge, was magical. There was a huge waterfall — two hundred feet tall — down the mountain to the west. It was quiet, green, and cool. When a storm was coming, you could see the dark clouds over the waterfall and feel the cold air come over the Alleghenies. Hardwood forests ran up the hill on both sides of the river, around old Indian caves in the side of the mountain. The deer and turkeys climbed up the banks of the river when it flooded and ate the vegetation that grew in the loose soil on the banks.

The springs that fed the river up in Bath County were clear and clean, full of life, trickling over the rocks. The paper mill had a dam built upriver in the seventies, flooding the old Indian caves. The water that flowed into Covington was clean and full of oxygen, but as soon as it hit the mill and the pollutants gushed in, it turned dark and foamy. From the paper mill downriver about ten miles, it was a dead zone. Then it fed into the Cowpasture River, and into the James River, and out into the Atlantic Ocean.

I'd heard a hundred times that the town would die without the mill. But the animals and fish were dying with it. An old man told me once that when they built the mill, the birds in Covington stopped singing. There weren't any left.

I looked deep into the woods and thought about Melinda's father, Buddy, who I barely remembered. My grandfather. Jimmy had told me that when Buddy was a young man, he left his small farm on the mountain every day before dawn with his dinner pail and his lantern and walked two miles down the mountain to a big farm in the valley near the river, where he worked the cornfields. Then those fields were flooded because of the dam.

I saw the herd of white cows that always stands in a grove of oaks on the hillside. The water had run down their bodies as the mist rose up from the heat — a ghostly, beautiful sight. The cows didn't mind the rain at all. They knew when it was coming, and they just let it come. Horses did this too, just hung their heads and let it pour. I wished I could be like that.

Then, as we came off the mountain, the lush farmland and forests turned into stores and parking lots and then the giant paper mill, leaking gray smoke out of more smokestacks than I could count. It looked like a plane had crashed into the valley, smoke curling up from all over the place into the sky. The rotten-egg stench was so powerful that it drifted for miles, up the Jackson River, through the hollows, to the most remote parts of the National Forest. It was an ungodly smell. Once in a while I saw tourists lost off the interstate driving through Covington with their shirts over their faces, like they were being suffocated. The smell was foul, sweet, irritating, and downright embarrassing.

The paper mill sat right in the middle of town. I knew if it wasn't for the mill, lots of people would have no place to work. But it sure was disgusting. Maybe they should leave and work somewhere else anyway, I thought. The mill took the best men we had and turned them into tired shift workers who never left Covington.

"When are you fixing my car?" I asked Wayne. I didn't even have my learner's permit yet, and my car had broken down twice. Wayne had gotten it for me from one of his horse-trader friends who I didn't trust one bit. Selling it to Wayne was probably cheaper than junking it.

"It's at your house."

"Thanks," I mumbled.

I was driving my father's pickup in the field when I was ten. Jimmy and Wayne would throw hay bales up on the back while I cruised down the rows. The sheriff was a friend of Wayne's, and he let me drive to the barn and back but nowhere else, which was stupid, but I guess that's what they have to do. I'm tall enough that I don't look too young behind the wheel, so sometimes I drive when I'm not supposed to and get away with it.

Wayne slowed down, and I felt a knot in my throat. He pulled into a church parking lot, swung the truck around back, and parked below a cemetery that stretched over a hill.

"I need to get home," I said.

"It's your daddy's birthday, and you know it."

He turned off the truck engine.

"Give him my respects," I said. I didn't feel like being there, and that was that.

Wayne walked around the truck and opened my door, but I stared straight ahead. Every time I looked up at that cemetery, I remembered Jimmy's funeral. I'd worn sneakers, but my mother didn't notice. Then I wore the same outfit to school three days in a row, and she still didn't say anything. I waited for her to start noticing me again.

I sat in the car for a minute or so, then gave up and got out, stiff and sore from my fall. I followed Wayne up the hill, watching his Red Wing boots sink into the mud up to the bottom of his coveralls.

As Wayne walked between the headstones, closer and closer to the grave, I thought about running the other way.

"You coming or what?" he said.

Jimmy had worked at one of the state fish hatcheries up in Montebello where they raised rainbow trout. When the fish were big enough, they loaded them up in a truck and stocked lakes and ponds all over the state of Virginia. I used to go with Melinda to visit him at his job. It was so quiet, no one around, just the vultures sitting in the trees over our heads waiting to scoop up a dead fish. I'd buy ten cents' worth of fish food from the machine — looked just like a gum dispenser — and toss the pellets into the dark water. The fish would grab the brown pellets gently. The young fingerlings would fight at the surface, not knowing there was more. The older fish knew there was always more. The job Jimmy had was a good one — didn't pay a whole lot, but he liked it.

Every year the town had a "Trout Derby," and Jimmy helped the kids stock the creek with fish. They'd jump into trucks and drive from one part of the creek to another, the boys and girls getting one fish each in a bucket. I rode with my father in the front of the state truck.

Once, Melinda and I went to visit Jimmy and he was taking a nap in that truck — up in the woods, sound asleep. I told Uncle Wayne about that, and he must have teased Jimmy a dozen times.

But my best memories of him were the trail rides. Every fall we'd load up a stock trailer with three horses and drive to West Virginia. Dozens of people came with their horses and camped out for three nights, sleeping in the cleaned-out stock trailers while their horses slept tied to trees. In the daytime we'd ride for hours through the woods, around peanut fields and cornfields, past cinder-block shacks and white clapboard churches. It was always hot and humid. Jimmy taught me how to tie a sponge to the saddle with a thin piece of rope. Whenever we crossed a stream, we'd drop the dry sponges down, hoist them up, and squeeze the cold water over the horses' withers. We'd walk the horses out of the woods at dusk, when the bobwhites would call from the edge of the swamp and the fireflies lit up the hay fields.

The deer flies would have stopped biting so much and the cicadas would be screaming from the woods as it got dark, and at night there'd be a dance with a real wooden dance floor and a country band, kegs of beer, and a big cookout. I'd watch my mother and father pass a flask of whiskey, and when they'd finally get up and start to slow dance, I'd walk back through the trailers, check the horses, crawl into my sleeping bag, and sleep so hard that when I woke up, I didn't know where I was.

Wayne and I stopped at a flat stone in the ground and looked.

JAMES CLORENT CRISER

1965–2009

For some stupid reason, it said "Daddy" under his name. I had been calling him Jimmy and my mama Melinda since I was two years old. He said I'd figured out that if I called them by their first names, they paid attention. Some lady at the tombstone company had talked Melinda into putting "Daddy" on it — Melinda was taking so many pills around then that she would have damn near run down the street naked if you said to. The stone was dirty now, and that made me angry at my mother. Jimmy Criser was neat and orderly, and everything he did, he did with care. All the time he'd spent making things right, and no one was keeping them up anymore. Was I supposed to do that too? Was I supposed to tell her what to put on the tombstone and how to keep it clean?

She'd given up on the tomato plants right away. Jimmy used to start thumbing through seed catalogs in February. Somebody had told him about a tomato called Radiator Charlie's Mortgage Lifter, after a mechanic who got out of debt by creating his own hybrid and selling the seedlings for a dollar apiece. Jimmy accidentally made his own hybrid after the wind mixed up the seeds he was storing by the shed. He'd crossed a green apple seed with some seeds of a fat orange tomato he'd gotten from grandma Elsie Cash, and he called the new tomato the Green Granny Cash. Once he was gone, Melinda didn't even tie up the tomato plants. They just tangled with the lamb's quarter in the yard.

Then Donald came. He ripped out the tomato plants and put grass seed down. He threw out all of Jimmy's stuff when I was at school. When I asked Melinda why, she said he felt like he wanted to make the family his own and that was a good thing. But I was sick over it. Everything was gone — pictures, clothes, records, magazines. I couldn't find anything of Jimmy's in the whole house. The only remnants were things at the barn. I figured that was all Jimmy had cared about in life anyway — his horse stuff — so I wouldn't let Wayne give any of that away. Not even a hoof pick.

After we'd stood by the grave a few moments, Wayne walked away. I started cleaning the stone with my finger, and Wayne came up behind me with a clean handkerchief.

I dipped it into a puddle and wiped around the letters, and then I scraped some dirt back and saw the horseshoe underneath Jimmy's name. I ran my thumb around the horseshoe.

As we walked back to the truck, the sun was setting.

"Your mama coming?" Wayne asked.

I didn't know what to say.

As if life wasn't hard enough, I had to drive by this damn cemetery every day. It would always be there, and he would always be in it. It made me sadder than anyone could imagine — that people wind up in the ground, and that's it. But sometimes I felt Jimmy watching, especially when Wayne and I were at the barn. I knew he'd like that red horse, the way that horse wasn't afraid of anything. I knew he'd argue with Wayne, tell him the horse could get some real money with a little work.

I tried not to cry as Wayne swung out into traffic, down the turnpike and past the farmer's co-op. The Blue Ridge Mountains rose up behind the paper mill like a big ocean wave about to overtake a rusty tanker. I wished the wave would sink the whole town and bury it on the ocean floor. I turned the radio on loud, but Wayne shut it off.

It was growing dark when Wayne pulled up in front of the house. The place looked terrible — the storm door was broken and swinging in the wind, bags of garbage were piled on the porch. My beat-up old car was parked in front.

"Thanks for my car," I said again. I pulled down the visor

and looked in the mirror. I had a fat lip and the beginning of a black eye.

"It'll do for now. Put some ice on your face," he said. "We'll get to work on that red horse tomorrow after school." He winked.

I got out and stopped at the metal gate. "You coming in?" I asked, knowing the answer.

"I'll strangle that bastard if I lay eyes on him."

I let the gate slam.

"Listen, you pay him no mind, you hear?" Wayne said. He seemed worried. I walked up on the porch, and he called after me. "He ain't worth your temper!"

He drove away.

FOUR

I STOOD ON THE porch for a little while, listening to Donald's voice. They didn't know I was there. I was waiting to see what kind of mood he was in. It was my father's birthday, and if Donald blew up at me, I wasn't sure what I would do.

I took a deep breath and walked into the house.

Melinda came out of the kitchen looking pale and tired. Her hair was dirty and she had on a stained sweatshirt. I could smell Windex — she cleaned when she got nervous. Donald was sitting on the couch polishing his new knife with his red bandana. He was one of those losers who felt like a man only when he was talking about his knives, polishing them, or reading about them in *Blade* magazine. I love a good knife, but it's a tool, for cutting open hay bales and whittling a stick. Not for pretending you're some kind of warrior.

Donald was skinny with a long face. He had heavy-lidded eyes, like a lizard. Some animal part of me saw him as a predator.

When I walked in, his little black eyes followed me. He had his dirty sock feet on my mother's maple coffee table. He'd never done that before.

I walked right past both of them.

Melinda saw my face and gasped. "What did you do?"

I kept walking.

"You don't answer your mama?" Donald said.

I stopped in my tracks. I could feel my face getting hot.

"Take those boots off and leave them outside," he ordered.

I looked down at my paddock boots. "They're not muddy," I said.

"You heard me!"

"How about you get your dirty feet off my mother's coffee table?"

My mother's face was frozen in fear. I headed for my room, and I was almost there before I felt his grip on my upper arm, pinching my skin.

"Let go," I said through my teeth, without turning around.

He tightened his grip. I yelped, and he released my arm. I knew he could snap my arm in two, and it scared me. I took my boots off and put them on the porch.

That was the first time he had ever laid a hand on me, and I don't think my mother breathed the entire time.

I went into my room, shut my door, and drove the wedge under it with my foot.

I had just stood there like a fool, not knowing what to do.

I barely recognized Melinda nowadays. A few months after Jimmy died, she had started including me in things again. She and I started going to McDonald's for pancakes every Saturday morning. We went camping up at Loft Mountain and looked for wildflowers, having a contest to see who could find more. I always won. I found some Indian Pipes the last time we went, and then Doll's Eye. I was pretty proud because only real hillbillies found Doll's Eye — the kind of mountain people who knew where the ginseng and the chanterelles grew but didn't tell anyone. I'd hoped we'd do all kinds of things together, like going on trips. Maybe one day we'd go to the beach. I'd always wanted to see the ocean.

But then about six months after Jimmy died, I woke up to find Donald in the living room. I had never seen him before. Apparently, Donald had flirted with Melinda at Food Lion the night before, when she was feeling down, and that was it — they went out and he came home with her. Melinda needed someone to be nice to her, and he knew just how to do that.

On the outside, Donald was a charmer. He was sugary sweet. He held doors for people, helped them with their bags, helped the neighbors chop firewood or get their trucks out of the snow, took loads of trash to the dump. Ladies said to me in town, "I'm so happy for your mother that she found someone so sweet" and "Isn't he wonderful?"

It was all fake. Donald did everything to make people like him, but it was a setup. He was laying the foundation so he could call anyone who crossed him crazy. Melinda bought the whole thing.

But I began to see what he was really like. He'd grab Melinda's arm hard enough to leave marks, and she'd get scared and pull away.

After that, I said something to one of Melinda's friends about what a nasty temper Donald had, and she said, "Honey, it sounds like you're jealous." One of my mother's old friends from Food Lion, Evelyn, was the only one who was suspicious of him. My mother wasn't allowed to talk to her anymore. Of course, Melinda wouldn't listen to me.

He was getting worse all the time. A few weeks back, when he sat down for dinner and saw a glass of water by his plate, he got up, grabbed Melinda by the hair, dragged her across the room, and shoved her out the front door. She came home fifteen minutes later with a bottle of Pepsi and apologized to him. *Apologized!* I felt like throwing up.

I picked up a *Practical Horseman* magazine to try to read about teaching a green horse how to jump. I had read that article over and over, and sometimes I just looked at the pictures of the horse trotting over the little cavalettis to make myself feel better. If you put those poles the right space apart, the horse'll trot right over them and not touch them. The horse in this article had a royal blue saddle blanket with white piping around the edges. I loved the way royal blue looked on a dark bay horse.

The walls of my room were covered with horse pictures of all of my favorite riders, but mostly George Morris. Wayne was the best horseman in the world, of course, but he was a horse trader to the bone, all about buying and selling. George was a classic horseman, a beautiful, elegant rider, and his students were the best. He mostly gave clinics nowadays, but he used to be the captain of the U.S. Olympic team. I studied pictures of him jumping horses over fences, how his hand had perfect contact through the reins, always a straight line to the horse's mouth. The stirrup was solidly on the ball of his foot, not stuck out on the toe the way many riders had it. He rode the horse, didn't pose or perch and try to look cool. His form meant something — he did it because it worked. George's book, *Hunter Seat Equitation,* never left my bedside table. It was tattered and stained and dog-eared from the hours I spent looking at the pictures of the master riders from twenty, thirty, fifty, years ago.

Hunt seat means English, the style used for fox hunting. *Equitation* just means good horsemanship. The idea is that a rider is always responsible for how a horse performs. You're not just there to look pretty and pose — you're there to get your horse over the fences as efficiently as possible. The best way to do that is to ride well. If your heels are down, your leg is tight. If you're sitting up tall, you're using your weight the right way. If you're stiff, your horse will get nervous. If your hands are soft, your horse will listen to them. Riding well looks good.

I was a practical rider. I never forced my heels down or closed my fingers because I was supposed to — I did it because it worked.

My other favorite riders were George's students who were on the U.S. Olympic team. Their students, and their students' students, all rode a little like George: functional, workmanlike, careful but daring at the same time. They were there to make the horse look good, and they gave every horse a different ride. I knew that some riders who won the big shows leased a horse from some rich person for a hundred thousand dollars and posed their way to a championship trophy.

I had one of George's sayings pinned up on the wall: "Perfection . . . like any good technique . . . becomes a defect. Perfection gets somebody self-conscious, which produces stiffness, a mechanical ride, a weak ride." I knew George would think I was a good rider, because perfection was the last thing I cared about. I was a rider who could ride anything. I'd ridden burros, mules, draft horses, ponies, racehorses, gaited horses. I'd driven a team, and I could drive four-in-hand by the time I was ten. I could jump a horse off a steep bank on a cross-country course, and I could gallop down a hill to a fence at the bottom.

The one thing I had never ridden was a "made" horse — a pushbutton, a horse that did everything for you. A made horse had been schooled until it was near perfect. You pointed him at the jump and he just jumped it. I couldn't imagine what it was like to rely on a horse this way. When I was riding a green horse, I felt like I had to damn near pick the horse up and carry him over the fence myself.

A made horse had been taught by the right trainers, the right way. He'd never had a bad rider on him. He'd never seen barbed wire or fought over hay with a dozen other horses. He'd spent his life moving from one clean nest of pine shavings to another. An expensive, insured, world-class horse that traveled by air, not cattle trailer. That was what I wanted to ride. The big German jumpers in the poster, with their crested necks standing square and catlike, tails cut bluntly below their hocks, as they lined up in the arena waiting for their trophies — they looked down at me and said, "Come get me!"

The riders on my walls smiled down at me in their show clothes — scarlet hunt coats, canary yellow vests, and shiny black field boots. A new pair of those show boots cost more than my car. I put down the magazine and flipped through the Dover Saddlery catalog to look at my favorite page, the dappled black bay horse handsomely modeling the plaid Baker turnout blanket. I wanted one of those for the red horse, but they cost almost two hundred dollars. The helmet all the equitation riders use, a GPA, was almost six hundred dollars. Der Dau field boots were eight hundred. Meanwhile, my mother and I were hiding from the meter reader and hoping he didn't cut off our electricity.

My room was a mess. I liked the idea of it being neat and clean, but some part of me wanted it messy. I liked the dirty clothes on the floor and the horse books everywhere. I liked it because it was mine. Sometimes I felt like a dog who brought things back to my dog bed, things no one else was allowed to touch. Sometimes I wanted to scratch around and curl up with all of my things and fall asleep, alone. Sometimes I wondered if I was a terrier in a former life, growling at people and scratching around for food.

I looked at the wedge in the door, a piece from an antique sewing table. Once, Melinda had a business as a seamstress. She tailored the uniforms that arrived by the vanful from the military institute over in Lexington. She could tailor those dress whites or those heavy wool dress blues with her eyes closed, and she'd made good money, especially right before graduation each year. She had four sewing machines in the basement, each one more beat-up than the last, but they were expensive and ran like tops. One day the institute hired its own seamstress on campus, and that was the end of it. Melinda said she wanted to start her own sewing store anyway — she was tired of the uniforms — and she looked for a storefront on Main Street in Clifton Forge. But then Jimmy died, and that was that. She got a job as a cashier at a grocery store.

Melinda had been a solid rider, although she didn't have any patience for a hot horse. She wanted something quiet, and she usually rode a quarter horse with a western saddle or a Morgan with a flat English one.

She hadn't liked it when Jimmy started buying horses off the track, especially when they needed fancy shoes and feed and the vet bills started racking up. But what really pushed her over the edge was the hunter mare from Warrenton that Jimmy bought for nine thousand dollars, the most he had ever paid for a horse. He had seen her in a farmer's field, thought he could get twenty thousand for her, and gambled all of their savings money. She was a cute and refined dapple gray with a sweet disposition. She had supposedly won the hunter stakes at the Warrenton horse show, then pulled a stifle muscle.

After six months of turnout, I started trotting her up and down hills every day for half an hour to strengthen her legs, but she was still lame. They put on five hundred dollars' worth of shoes, shot her hocks up with cortisone, and gave her bute every day in her feed. Didn't help. X-rays, vet bills — still lame. Finally, a new vet said she had degenerative hock disease and would always be lame.

By then, Jimmy was out seventeen thousand dollars, and

my parents had nothing left. I had spent every day working the mare, so none of the other horses were exercised. The vet refused to come for any other horses until Jimmy paid the bill, so he sold the tractor and took care of it. Then they were living paycheck to paycheck, bills weren't getting paid, and they had no tractor to make hay. Jimmy started asking for favors everywhere, and it nearly broke Melinda, who was proud as hell and never asked for nothing.

FIVE

AFTER A WHILE, my mother knocked on the door, but I ignored her. She kept knocking.

"Sidney, it's me." She lowered her voice to a whisper. "You okay?"

Whispering in her own house.

She knocked again, harder, and I pulled out the wedge.

Melinda opened the door and looked at my face. "You fall off?"

I nodded.

"He certainly didn't mean to hurt your feelings."

"Poor Donald," I said.

"Don't be so difficult. And stop fighting with everybody."

"If that man ever touches me again, I'll kill him. I swear to God."

"Honey, you have got to stop provoking people. Some people just cannot handle it."

Melinda sat down on the bed, but I moved away from

her. Ever since she'd started seeing Donald, I hadn't wanted her to get too close. Now I couldn't even look at her.

"They cut all my hours," she said.

"That's your problem."

"It's *our* problem."

I wondered if she had any problems that were just hers.

She got up and went to the door.

"Today is Jimmy's birthday," I said.

"I know. I was going over to the cemetery," she said.

It was a lie, and we both knew it.

"What are we gonna do about money?" she asked instead.

"You're asking me?" I said.

"I'm looking for a job." She hesitated. "Donald might loan me money for rent, so please don't pick any more fights with him."

"You ain't taking money from him."

"We need his help right now." She looked desperate.

"If we had money, would you make him leave?"

She didn't answer.

"You would. You'd get rid of him," I said. My heart was pounding.

"I never said that."

But I could see it.

"I'm going to sell this horse with Wayne," I said.

"What horse?" Melinda said, spitting out the word *horse* like tobacco juice.

"You'll see."

"Another goddamn horse, eating money."

She left.

I looked outside at the shiny grille of Donald's truck leering at me like a big set of teeth.

One time I'd told Uncle Wayne that Donald was dumb. "Dumb like a fox," he said. "I tell you one thing — he might be a mean son of a bitch, but he ain't no fool." I knew that now, and I wanted him gone. In another state with no forwarding address. In jail. Anything.

When I used to go to church with my father, we always knelt and asked for forgiveness. Now I knew the things I was thinking about Donald might be wrong, but I couldn't ask for forgiveness because I wasn't sorry. Jimmy had always said to open my heart and treat people with love when things were bad. But I couldn't. I wondered how open my father's heart would be if he were here and saw what I saw. Maybe the Bible and the prayer for forgiveness were luxuries for those who didn't have evil at their door.

My mind wandered to the red horse, how he had strong legs and dense bones like an Arabian. What that meant on the track or in the show ring was that he could go for a long time without getting tired or sore. Those Arabs could go for a hundred miles in the desert. For some reason the

Thoroughbred breeders ignored the soundest horses, breeding one famous Thoroughbred racehorse to another until they were too overbred and their worst traits were exaggerated. They might be fast, but their legs were frail, or they were bird-brained and skittish. Or they colicked easily. Or their hooves fell apart during the rainy season. Instead of finding some hearty Arabian blood, or a draft horse, or even a quarter horse, those ignorant breeders would just breed one Thoroughbred to another and make it worse.

When I looked at the red horse, I saw something else, and I knew that somewhere in his family tree was a very strong, sound horse. The kind you could count on. And somewhere in a file cabinet in a tack room in an old barn, probably locked with a missing key, were this red horse's papers, dusty and stuck together. Maybe I could find them. Maybe I could make all the money back that Jimmy had lost on the gray mare. Sometimes things can turn around fast.

SIX

When I opened my eyes in the morning, I knew immediately that summer was over. The thought pushed down on my chest like a ton of bricks. I got dressed and left the house before I had to speak to anyone. I started my car, turned on the country music station, and took off.

From the parking lot I walked up to the ugly concrete-box high school. The school seemed huge compared to junior high. Seeing other kids get out of their cars was weird. I saw the cluster of rich rednecks. And the jocks. And a few hillbillies. The kids looked tanner and older than they had last May, and they didn't make eye contact with me. I didn't see Ruthie or anyone else I knew, and I didn't care. The sooner I got out of this place, the better. I wasn't there to make friends.

My first class was English with Ms. Cash, who frowned at me like a bulldog. I'd had her in eighth grade, too, plus she was kin to my father. Boy, I hated English. I usually read the first couple of chapters and faked the rest.

After class, I was walking out the door when I heard Ms.

Cash growl my name. "Sidney Criser, I would like to talk to you."

I turned around.

"You plan on working this year?"

I didn't answer.

Ms. Cash waited for the other kids to leave. "A lot of these nimrods can barely read a newspaper."

I was surprised she said that, and I laughed.

"But they still do the damn reading. Maureen will probably be pregnant a year from now and married to that idiot. But she'll still have read *As I Lay Dying.*" Ms. Cash tightened her mouth and sank into her snarly mountain voice. "Too hard, Sidney?"

"No ma'am, it's not too hard."

"Then read it."

I nodded and walked away. Shit. First class of the year.

At lunchtime, I went to the cafeteria and grabbed an empty table. The rich kids sat at one table, the trailer-park kids at another. The sons and daughters of the local judges, lawyers, and doctors sat at their own table. They wanted to go to private schools, but there weren't any around, and boarding school meant boarding school. They didn't look at anyone, much less talk to them.

I finally saw Ruthie. Her dark hair was pulled into a messy ponytail as usual, and her cheap blue sweater had little fuzz balls all over it.

When she saw my black eye, her mouth fell open. "You get in a fight?"

"Yeah. With a horse."

The big Martin boy who lived in Low Moor whistled loudly, and I looked at him. He was staring right at me.

"Hey, come sit with me, girl!"

Ruthie glanced at him nervously, and then we ignored him. He was cute, but I would never tell anyone I thought that. I had seen him once at Walmart, and after he winked at me, I couldn't look him in the eye ever again. He was a lot less cute when he was driving around in his jacked-up Ford F-250, revving his engine. As long as these were the boys that me and Ruthie saw on a daily basis, we would never, ever lose our virginity.

Eileen Cleek, whose hair was cut short and boyish, stopped by our table. She had a deep farmer's tan from working on her dad's cattle farm all summer with her four brothers. Everyone thought she was a lesbian, including me, but Eileen didn't care. She was as tough as they come.

"Your uncle Wayne sold my daddy a Percheron mare that could pull the goddamn *Titanic,*" she said. "Strongest horse I ever saw."

"Hope you got a good deal," I said.

"From your uncle? Not quite."

I smiled.

Eileen walked on. She would definitely work at her family farm once she got out of high school. Eileen was the only person I'd ever seen who was like me.

Ruthie was looking over her homework.

"My mom got laid off," I said.

"Shit," she said.

"*Shit*'s right."

"What are you going to do?"

"I'm going to try to sell this horse with Uncle Wayne and make a couple thousand. Then we can get Donald out of the house, once and for all."

"You think your mama wants him out?"

"I'm gonna get him out whether she does or not," I said.

One of the rednecks yelled at me, "How'd you get that black eye, girl?"

"Beating up assholes like you," I said.

His friends laughed. Ruthie ignored them. "You could go work in the mill with Daddy," she said.

"I think I'm a little young for mesothelioma. Then again, maybe you're never too young."

I knew what she was thinking. The kids here thought they'd be lucky to get a job at the mill when they graduated.

"What are you going to do after high school?" Ruthie asked.

"I'm going to be a catch rider."

"What's that?"

"Catch riders go to horse shows and people pay them to ride their horses. They can ride anything."

Ruthie looked at me like I was crazy. "See you in class," she said. She got up and dumped her trash into the garbage can.

As Ruthie left the lunchroom, two girls laughed at her, and she walked away from them as fast as she could. I got up and went over to the girls. One of them was tall with dyed blond hair and bad posture. The other one was a stumpy little cheerleader with tight jeans and pink lip-gloss. They got worried when they saw me coming with my black eye and fat lip.

"You're just friends with her because you feel sorry for her," said the tall one.

"You gonna be the one people feel sorry for," I said.

"Oh, please. Who beat you up, your daddy or your mama?"

I balled up my fist and pushed it against the tall one's chest. "You laugh at Ruthie again, you'll look worse than I do."

The tall girl froze, and her friend scurried away.

I couldn't stand anyone being nasty to Ruthie. She wouldn't hurt a fly. One day in middle school she had seen me eating by myself, and she'd sat down. I guess I glared at her, and she looked so scared that I felt awful. We ate without talking for a few minutes.

"You make me laugh in math," she said. "You're all sarcastic to those popular girls, and I have to pinch myself so I don't crack up."

"Well, they're dumb as dog shit. If I don't make fun of 'em, I'll strangle 'em," I said.

Ruthie snorted and grabbed her nose in embarrassment. I laughed. After that, we ate lunch together every day.

When I went to school after Jimmy died, no one knew what to say, so no one said anything. I had thought people would be nice to me, but having a dead parent just made you weirder. Ruthie understood this, even though her mother had been dead a long time. That was why Ruthie had found the guts to talk to me in the first place. It was our club, the only club we could join, the only place we felt welcome.

I went back to the table to finish my lunch alone. I looked at the vast room full of kids laughing, talking, and taunting each other, the blinking fluorescent lights, the missing ceiling tiles. These kids were never going anywhere. They'd either be drunk and unemployed or drunk and collecting a paycheck from the paper mill.

I had to get out of there, and the first step was selling that red horse.

SEVEN

After school, I drove to Wayne's. I pulled into his dirt driveway, parked, and got out. I had a spring in my step just thinking about how we were going to start working the red horse. Maybe we'd just trot him clockwise, or we could do figure eights to loosen up his shoulders, but I didn't want to make him ring-sour. I finally decided I was going to ride him in the lower field where it was flat. We'd take walks on the trails and around the hay fields. That way, he wouldn't get bored.

I saw Wayne next to the shed, picking the horse's feet. I was glad he already had him out of the field.

"Melinda got laid off," I said.

Wayne examined the bottom of the horse's hoof, then put it down. He stood up straight and looked at me.

"He stepped on a wood staple," he said.

I picked up the horse's foot and looked underneath. I saw the tiny hole, then I saw the long wood staple in Wayne's hand, and I knew it had gone in deep.

"Must have happened last night in the field," said Wayne. "He's lame. We gotta dig that hoof out, pack it, bandage it, and lay off for at least six weeks. Got to soak it every day in Epsom salts, pack it with iodine."

The horse wouldn't put much weight on that foot. His head hung low, and his ears drooped sadly to the sides.

I felt sick. Rage boiled inside me and I felt like I couldn't breathe. I looked at the barbed wire, the rusty barrels, and the broken tractor with weeds growing around it. I picked up a blacksmith's hammer and hurled it into the side of the shed, leaving a deep dent.

"Hey!" Wayne yelled.

"Maybe if you cleaned up this place, he wouldn't have stepped on a wood staple! Looks like a hillbilly lives here!"

I tried not to cry but I just couldn't help it. Sub was standing there, his lower lip hanging loosely like an old man's. I looked at his calm, strong face and cursed at him.

"That was your daddy's horse, Sid."

Wayne chewed on a toothpick, thinking. "One of the men quit at the barn. You want to come work there?"

I thought he was kidding me. "At Oak Hill? Cleaning stalls for those rich kids?"

"You think you're too fancy?"

"The last thing I need is a bunch of snotty girls bossing me around while I shovel their horses' shit."

"Come right after school, and work on the weekends," he said.

He was serious. He thought I would ride with him all the way over to Crozet to clean stalls. I knew he did it three times a week, and I figured that was his penance for being a drunk and not having a plan for his life. Damned if I was going to be his age and working as a stable hand. I wasn't going to do it at fourteen, either.

Wayne sliced open a bale of hay with his pocketknife. "You want to make some money or not?"

"I don't need to make money that way. I make money riding and selling."

"Listen, Sidney. Your grandma got up at four thirty in the morning to shovel stalls before school, rode all day afterward."

He was full of shit and I knew it. "I thought she was a catch rider."

"She was." His voice was loud and sharp, and he straightened up and looked me right in the eye. I could tell he was going to let me have it.

"She could ride any horse you got — I don't care if it was a show hunter or a donkey or a Budweiser Clydesdale. She might have been poor, but she would iron her riding clothes until they were perfect, shine her boots, and go to a horse show, and them owners would be fighting each other to pay her to ride their horses. And when she rode, she won. You know how she learned all this? By working her ass off, night and day."

"I work my ass off here with you."

He looked at me, smiled, and let out a big guffaw. "You think so, do you? Be here tomorrow after school. Three o'clock."

I started up my engine with a roar and kicked up dirt as I left.

Driving home, as the sky grew dark, I looked at the paper mill, the smokestack lights blinking, like a ship on the ocean. As the shift changed, workers filed in and out like robots. I pulled over and watched them, wondering what it would be like to have a paycheck put right into my bank account. It would be great to get Donald out, and my mother would be so happy, whether she knew it or not. I saw a girl a little older than me walk out and get into a new truck. She drove past me, laughing into her cell phone.

I stayed up that night and read a little, just to get Ms. Cash off my back. The book was weird. It told you what was in every character's mind. I wondered if you really should feel empathy for some of these lowlifes. If you saw things through everyone else's eyes, the world would be a house of mirrors. It was confusing, and I fell asleep.

EIGHT

THE NEXT DAY at school, I sat through my classes thinking about whether I would go to Oak Hill with Wayne. I couldn't learn anything new from shoveling more manure. It was all the same, whether it came from a fancy show jumper or an old mule.

When I passed by the main office on my way out the door, I saw Eileen Cleek being lectured by the assistant principal. "Eileen, you miss more than two weeks of school this year, you ain't going to graduate."

"Don't tempt me," Eileen said.

I laughed, and Eileen winked at me, walked outside after me, and headed for her beat-up Chevy truck. A couple of boys yelled "Lesbo" at her. She swore at them, and for the first time, I felt a little sorry for her. She was always alone. No one really cared whether she liked boys or girls — people just got angry because they couldn't figure it out.

Wayne had never told me much about Oak Hill, just that

the horses were fancy and the people were rich. He said they went to big shows and won lots of trophies. That was about it; for some reason, he didn't like to talk about it. Maybe they were mean to him there. Maybe I'd have to set them straight.

When I pulled in to Wayne's place, I was late, but he was waiting in his truck. I turned off the car and we looked at each other.

"What do I bring?" I asked.

"Just yourself."

"I gotta get my saddle."

"You need your saddle to clean stalls?"

I slid out of the car, walked around his truck, and got in.

"What're they paying?"

"Minimum."

I sighed.

"That's more per hour than you're making now," he said.

We got on the interstate and hit about eighty in that old truck of his. He said it was ninety miles — through Bath County, Allegheny, Rockbridge, and into Albemarle.

He told me that he slept in the barn sometimes, got up and worked there the next day, which I never knew. I said I wasn't sleeping in their goddamn barn — they could put me up in a hotel. For some reason, he thought that was hilarious.

The truck heaved up Afton Mountain and started down the other side. There was so much fog on the top of the mountain that tractor-trailers were pulled over, hazards flashing. As Wayne came over the top, the fog thinned, and I could see the cars in front of us again.

I looked at the white rock formations peeking through the exposed bluffs on top of the mountain. Ruthie's dad, Earl, had told me it was quartzite, one of the toughest rocks in the world. He had been working in the Massey Mine in Highland County when Ruthie lost her mother, and he'd quit and gotten a job at the mill because Ruthie and her sister were scared that they might lose him, too. But he was a miner at heart, knowing every rock and vein in Allegheny County.

One time, when we were little, he took Ruthie, Dorine, and me down near the Trueheart Mine in Amelia County in the early spring to look for gems in the rich, red clay. Amelia was on a fault line, ripe for rock hounds. We had packed a lunch and a couple of sodas and driven through the mountains, then through the tobacco fields lined with Queen Anne's lace and barbed wire, and then we'd turned off the main road and gone deep into the woods. Ruthie's father had pulled up to a white farmhouse and slipped a dollar bill under the door as payment for rock hunting. It was spooky. There was no one around but a deerhound covered in fat yellow ticks.

We'd dug our shovels into the silty creek bed, put a clump of dirt onto the screen, and hosed it off. I found a piece of shiny black tourmaline the size of my finger wedged into a rock, and when Ruthie's father saw it, he whistled. Over the years, he'd found dozens of aquamarines, amethysts, buckets full of smoky quartz, but this was something rare. He told me to keep it just like it was because God had taken his time with it. I was surprised when he said this — he wasn't usually that sentimental. But it gave me a tingly feeling down my back because he said it like he meant it, and for a split second I thought it might be true. If God, whoever that was, took his time with a piece of tourmaline, why the hell didn't he bring my father home from the Falling Springs market?

"These rich people are just like you and me," Wayne finally said, interrupting my thoughts. "They put their boots on one at a time, just like we do." He sounded like he was trying to convince himself.

After we passed Shadwell, we took the Crozet exit. The spiny mountains rolled into hills with thick, wet pasture lined with black fencing. Horses grazed in clusters below barns on distant hilltops. The grass was bright green, no bare spots or patches of tall weeds. It was like green carpet that someone had laid out and stapled right up to the fence posts.

I hadn't been on this side of Afton Mountain in a while. When we looked for horses, we usually traveled the other way, toward West Virginia. Two Olympians from the U.S. Equestrian Team had come from near Charlottesville, and I wondered if I might meet someone who knew them. I'd read about Melvin Poe, the huntsman of Orange County Hunt, how he'd taken Jackie Kennedy out fox hunting. I pictured Melvin dressed in a pink coat and canary vest, flask in his pocket, dented hunting horn in his hand.

"Who owns the barn?" I asked Wayne.

"Mr. and Mrs. Wakefield. They owned the paper mill before they sold it."

"*The* paper mill?"

He nodded. "Their daughter, Dee Dee, is at the barn a lot with her daughter, Kelly, who you oughta steer clear of."

"Why?" I asked.

"She ain't no good."

I was going to ask him why and tell him I wasn't steering clear of anyone — she could steer clear of me — but for some reason I decided not to.

NINE

WAYNE SLOWED DOWN at a sign that read OAK HILL above a fox head and hunting horn, and he turned in. I grew anxious, and my eyes searched the fields around us. We drove up a long driveway to a two-story stone barn. A stable hand was raking the pea gravel in the driveway, and another one was weeding planters overflowing with red verbena. I got out of the truck and jammed my hands into my pockets. I'd never walked into a barn before without bringing my saddle and chaps.

A Mexican stable hand in his forties nodded at Wayne and looked at me. He carried himself like a barn manager, checking the horses, watching what the other grooms were doing.

"Whatever you do, you don't talk to that lazy son of a bitch," Wayne said to me loudly. The man turned and smiled.

This meant that the man was someone I could trust. The meaner the insult, the closer the friend. Sure enough, Wayne winked and told me that was Edgar, one of the grooms.

The barn was all oak with brass fixtures. I had never seen anything like it before. There wasn't a speck of hay or sawdust in the aisle. A brass nameplate was attached to the door of each stall. SUMMER BREEZE. LADY GAGA. DANCING BEAR. I saw a big gray hunter resting his chest against a nylon stall guard with his head way out in the aisle. I saw some Welsh ponies and what looked like Thoroughbreds. Each one was clipped and clean — I mean, not even an inch of a whisker. No hair in the ears, no dirt, nothing. I'd never been in a barn that barely smelled like a barn.

Mexican grooms were cleaning stalls, clipping, wrapping legs, and feeding. They talked quietly to one another in Spanish and moved around the horses with ease.

I followed Wayne down the aisle.

In one stall I saw a black bay Thoroughbred, standing up and sound asleep. On his blanket was his name in script: KATAHDIN. The aisle between the rows of stalls was lined with monogrammed fiberglass tack trunks.

I walked by the open tack room and looked in, smelling glycerin saddle soap and neat's-foot oil. Two grooms were cleaning dirty bridles hanging from a hook. They wiped their sponges across the translucent gold bars of soap in a quick rhythm. I could see from across the room that the bridles were made of English leather, not the cheap Indian leather that was already dark brown when it was brand-new and tore after only a year.

Wayne handed me a pitchfork and wheelbarrow and pointed to a row of stalls. A metal bowl with a cone on the bottom was bolted inside the first stall, and I asked Wayne what it was.

"Automatic watering system," he said.

I'd read about these but had never seen one in real life. When a horse drank all the water, the metal bowl filled up on its own. I just stared at it, thinking about the hours and hours I'd spent — in the heat, in ice storms, you name it — filling up water buckets. "Do they freeze?"

"Hell no, they don't freeze," he said. "They're heated."

"So nobody here ever has to break the ice in the water buckets," I said.

"Nope. And if the horse wants fresh water, he just pushes that knob with his nose," he said. I guess he saw me wondering why we didn't have that system. "These things cost about three hundred dollars each, and don't even ask how much it is to do the plumbing and 'lectricity."

He gestured to the wheelbarrow, letting me know we had to stop talking and work, and disappeared down the aisle. I pulled the wheelbarrow up to the first empty stall and shoveled hard.

Two girls a little older than me came around the corner in polo shirts, riding breeches, and black boots, and I peeked out at them through the bars. Their riding clothes were dirty, and their spurs were still fastened to their boots. They were tall and thin, with long shiny hair pulled into ponytails. One had thick blond streaks from the sun and wore a green shirt. She didn't have much makeup on. She had no expression on her face and an upside-down mouth, like a fish, and she walked like a jock. The other one had dark hair and looked a little friendlier.

"My mom bought that gelding," said the dark-haired one.

"What?" said the blond one.

"I know — she's crazy. She must have been on Klonopin."

"He's totally green. She can't ride him."

"She paid fifty thousand dollars for him," said the dark-haired one.

"Oh my God." The blond one giggled loudly.

"She didn't even ask my dad."

I waited for them to go by, but they stopped a few feet away.

"Is that Scotty's new turnout blanket?" the blonde asked. "It's green and blue."

"Those are my horse's colors."

"I guess now they're hers, too. She is such a copycat," said the blonde.

"She's moving him to another barn this week. Thank God."

I pushed the wheelbarrow, piled high with manure, out of the stall. The girls looked me up and down, said squirrelly little "hi"s, and watched me go by. I dumped the wheelbarrow into the manure pile, filled it up with sawdust, and pushed it back down the aisle past them. It was squeaking loudly, and I could feel them staring at me. I heard one of them murmur something. When I looked up at them, they smiled a little too hard.

Suddenly, a man's voice boomed down the aisle. "Are your horses cooled and washed, tack cleaned?"

"We were just — " the tall one started.

"Did you cool that horse off or just throw him in his stall? And did you put ointment in the pony's eye?"

The other girl was cowering. "Sorry, Dutch."

I froze. Had she really said "Dutch"?

A tall middle-aged man rounded the corner. It was *the* Dutch Thompson, who coached all the top equitation riders in the area. He always had a few riders in the finals. Equitation is a small world — it's junior riders only, under eighteen, and it's judged on the rider, not the horse. I'd never been in an equitation class in a horse show. But I knew I could compete in one if I wanted to. It was just a test of horsemanship, and I was a better horseman than any of these girls.

I'd been reading about Dutch Thompson for years. I'd seen at least fifty pictures of him coaching, I'd watched videos of his clinics, I'd read his column in *The Chronicle of the Horse*. I knew his horses' names from back when he used to compete in Grand Prix jumping events around the world. I knew what color breeches he wore and how he rode with his lower leg a little bit forward like they did on a fox hunt. I knew that he grew up in The Plains, Virginia, and that he spent every winter on the Florida circuit.

But I didn't know Wayne worked for him. That dumb old man had told me all this time that he was "working at some show barn" in Crozet, and when I'd asked him the details, he'd just said, "Ponies." What a fool. I wanted to go find him, but I couldn't move because Dutch Thompson was staring me down like he was going to eat me. He was polished, all business, in clean khakis and a striped oxford shirt with the sleeves rolled up. In that outfit, he looked like he was working in an office, not running a barn.

"That horse gets peanut hulls. Didn't you see that?" he said sharply, towering over me and watching me with hawk eyes. I was too scared to answer.

He pointed to a chalkboard on the wall, then over at the horses.

"This horse gets straw in his stall, this one sawdust. Water bowls are scrubbed every day with Betadine." He looked around — for a groom, I guessed. "Is someone training this girl?"

Dutch walked to another stall, slid the door open, and examined a chunky chestnut. He rested his hand on the horse's chest to see if he had a fever, pulled the horse's lip up, pressed into his gums, and watched the color return to the thumbprint. He caught me watching him.

"I need those stalls done. We're bringing horses in," he said coldly.

I started shoveling fast, sweating. I cleaned one stall, then another. I felt like it was taking forever. At one point, I knocked into the wheelbarrow handle and dumped it over, spilling sawdust into the aisle.

"Here's what you do." I turned and saw Wayne looking at me through the bars.

"You could have told me this was Dutch Thompson's barn."

"You heard of him?" Wayne said.

"Yeah, I heard of him. He's famous."

Wayne shrugged.

"I have two more stalls," I said.

"First get rid of the wet bedding. Then take whatever is dirty but dry and stomp it down into the wet spot to soak it up."

"You done with yours?"

He nodded and pushed his steel-tipped boot down into the straw, which soaked up the urine. I could tell he'd done this a thousand times.

When we were finished cleaning, I followed Wayne outside along a fence line toward the upper fields. We passed Dutch giving a lesson to a girl on a pony, trotting back and forth over a wooden pole on the ground.

"See that pony tossing his head?" asked Wayne. "He's out

of patience, and in a minute he's gonna get ornery. He wants to jump."

Sure enough, the pony put his head down and bucked. "Pull his head up!" Dutch yelled to the rider.

"You don't think Dutch knows what he's doing?" I asked Wayne.

"Not if you ask me. Or that pony." He reconsidered. "Well, he do and he don't," he admitted. "He knows how to win."

We walked up the hill toward an old brick mansion surrounded by boxwood hedges.

"The Wakefields live there," said Wayne.

Wayne gave me a halter and lead rope, and he rattled the gate loudly. Hearing the sound, a group of tall, muscular horses in their paddocks lumbered over the hill toward us. Glistening in the sun, they stomped their feet impatiently, ready to go in and eat dinner. They were well fed, lean, and strong. Wayne glanced at me to see my reaction. I had never seen horseflesh like this.

"We got two Danish Warmbloods, a Thoroughbred, and a Hanoverian mare," Wayne said proudly. "And a half-Shire, half-Thoroughbred gelding."

He gestured toward a dark dapple gray. "That there's an Oldenburg gelding," he continued. "Get too close and he will bite the living hell outta you."

The big horse extended his neck and snapped at me, and

I pushed his cheek away. "That horse must be seventeen and a half hands," I said.

"He jumps big, too," Wayne said.

"We each get three?"

"Naw . . . they don't like us walking back more than two horses at a time."

"Why not? That's stupid."

"Honey, that German horse must be worth a coupla hundred thousand dollars all by himself."

"God Almighty," I said.

I looked at the German horse. He had a lazy, bored look and a big green stain on his flank.

"So you'd better do a good job getting that shit stain off his belly."

We walked back leading one horse each and made the trip two more times, turning the big horses loose in their nice, clean stalls, where they rooted around in the white pine shavings. I tied up the massive gray horse in the wash stall. As I hosed him down, he showed his big teeth and pink gums. I laughed at him as he tried to bite the water like a dog.

"Careful — don't get water in his ears. He'll turn into Satan himself."

I turned to see a boy, maybe about eighteen, with his hands in his pockets. He wore a baseball cap and an old Wilson's Feed and Seed T-shirt. He was a little skinny, with hazel eyes and light brown hair. I was embarrassed at the way I looked, sawdust all over my pants, and I tried to brush my hair out of my face.

"Is he yours?" I asked.

He shook his head. "I spotted him as a baby, and they bought him really cheap. The seller thought he was permanently lame, but it was just a pulled muscle. He's fine now."

"He's got some big feet," I said.

"You don't have to tell me!" He laughed. "Nearly broke my foot last week, big dumb bastard. Watch this."

He scratched the horse under his belly, and the horse stuck his neck out and lifted his lip, enjoying it.

"I'm Wes," the boy said.

"Sid."

"You from around here?" he asked.

"Near Covington."

"That's a ways away," he said. "I don't know how anyone lives there with the smell of the paper mill."

"You get used to it," I lied. "Where you from?"

"I grew up in Nelson County."

"Where?" I asked.

"Massies Mill."

I remembered a fat Shetland pony I'd seen with Wayne over in Massies Mill. The owner had told Wayne the horse was ten, but when we got there, we could tell across the paddock that the pony was about thirty years old.

"Why are you laughing?" he asked.

"I thought only pigs and chickens lived in Massies Mill," I said.

He looked a little hurt and I felt stupid. I had just been trying to be funny.

"We had pigs," he said. "Also horses, cows, guineas, and everything in between."

"Your daddy is a pig farmer? Really?"

"And a blacksmith and a carpenter. Whatever pays."

"My uncle's like that," I said.

He sure acted different from the boys his age at school.

"Where do you go to school?" I asked him.

"Nelson County High School, in Lovingston. I'm a junior."

I was just about to tell him proudly that Wayne was my uncle when the tall girl in the green shirt from before walked around the corner. She came up behind Wes and put her arms around him. He turned, looking startled, and she kissed him. Right on the mouth.

"Hi, Kelly," he said.

I felt a knot in my stomach that made me embarrassed all over again. Kelly ignored me as I finished washing the gelding. "How was school?" he asked her.

"Whatever. Another exciting day at St. Elizabeth's."

She tilted her head, gathered her hair on one side, and twirled her little earring between her thumb and forefinger.

"Can you get her horse tacked up, Wes?" barked a short-haired woman of about fifty, overtanned, with the same fish mouth as Kelly's. "I want her to be warmed up before the lesson starts."

"Yes, Dee Dee," he answered.

"I didn't know you were coming, Mom," muttered the girl.

I noticed that Dee Dee was wearing a diamond bracelet. In the barn.

"I'm watching your lesson, Kelly," Dee Dee said.

Kelly looked like all the air had been sucked out of her. She hunched her shoulders and exchanged a look with Wes.

I put the gray horse into his stall, and Kelly followed me. "Make sure you put extra shavings in here around the edges," she told me. "This horse gets stuck against the wall while he's sleeping and can't get up. It's really dangerous —"

"Cast," I said.

"What?"

"He gets cast in his stall. That's the word."

"I know," said Kelly defensively. She looked me up and down and walked away, slinging a lead rope over her shoulder.

"Who is that?" Dee Dee asked her, gesturing toward me.

"I don't know."

I watched some of Kelly's lesson through the bars on the

windows. She was jumping an elegant chestnut back and forth over a vertical in the middle of the ring, and Dutch's voice boomed throughout the ring and the barn.

"Move him up," he said after one jump.

She circled around and came back the other way.

"Make him bend," Dutch said. "Go wide and jump in easy . . ."

"Move him up" meant make him go faster or make his strides longer so that he covered more ground. "Make him bend" meant that the horse should use his whole body in the turns. When a horse bent through the turn, he had his rear end up under him and was using all his strength. If he was balanced right, he'd jump better. Some people called this "setting him up." I'd never heard anyone say "jump in easy," but I guessed that it meant get in a little closer.

I watched Kelly move the horse up, jump in too easy, and pull a rail off the vertical.

"Not spur, leg. Just leg," Dutch said. "And I wouldn't be afraid to ask him for his leads."

The lead was which front leg came first at a canter. If you picture a horse running around a turn, of course he'd want the inside leg coming first. Having the outside leg come first is called a "counter-canter," otherwise known as "the wrong lead." They made you counter-canter in an equitation class. Not too many of the horses we broke at Wayne's would hold a counter-canter. They weren't well schooled enough.

Dutch set up a course of eight fences, and Kelly rode the course. I had to work, so I couldn't watch all of it, but I saw a couple of other girls watching Kelly's lesson like she was some kind of celebrity. At one point, Kelly's horse slammed on the brakes and refused a fence, and she had to circle around and keep trying.

When the lesson was over, Kelly walked the horse back toward the barn. Dee Dee was following, scolding her. "You're relying on the number of strides and not your eye."

"Why did you keep talking about moving up and making it five strides, then?" Kelly asked. "You say that, and then you say to use my eye!"

"Did you get anything out of that lesson?" Dee Dee asked.

"I would have if you hadn't been there!" Kelly said. She sounded like she was about to cry.

I ducked down to make sure they couldn't see me.

All this time, Wes was exercising a horse in a warm-up ring. He never muscled the horse with his strength, like many men do. He trotted a gelding over low jumps, patting him on the neck. The horse looked very green, barely broke.

Kelly and one of her friends came up behind me and saw me watching Wes. I didn't know the other girl's name — they all looked exactly alike with their buff breeches, field boots, alligator shirts, and ponytails. Kelly seemed upset, and I felt sorry for her. I thought about saying something, decided not to, but then a flicker of goodwill passed over me.

"I saw some of your lesson," I said. "You did a nice job."

"Don't watch my lesson," she said with her lip back, showing a row of perfect white teeth. The look on her face was so angry that I just stood there and stared. "You're supposed to be cleaning stalls," she said.

She looked at her friend and they laughed at me, like it was a joke.

"I ride, too, you know," I said.

They laughed even harder.

"She rides, too!" Kelly said. "What do you ride?"

"Hunters."

They kept laughing. Kelly put her hand on the side of the barn to hold herself up. "She rides hunters." Kelly put her other hand on her chest as if she was having a heart attack.

Her friend wheezed and held her side, as if she'd never heard anything as funny as what I'd said.

I imagined stuffing their pretty faces into the dirty stall next to me, manure stuck in their lip-gloss.

I knew they couldn't do half the things I'd done.

TEN

DURING THE LONG ride home, I wanted to kick myself for trying to be nice to Kelly. Why the hell did I think I needed to prove myself to her? Who gave a shit what she thought? I was too angry and humiliated to tell Wayne what had happened. He would just make it worse. He'd warned me, and I was already ignoring his advice. Something inside me had lit on fire when those girls had laughed at me, and it wasn't a good thing. Wayne would tell me to go in there, clean stalls, and keep my mouth shut.

I asked Wayne what those girls were doing at Oak Hill. He told me they were trying to qualify for the Maclay Finals by winning points in Maclay classes, held at big horse shows. I had read about the Maclay competition many times and stared at pictures of the winning horses and riders in *Practical Horseman* for years. I had imagined Maclay riders as nice girls who had worked hard to get there and the horses as their best friends, but it wasn't turning out that way. It looked like these bitchy girls were buying the best horses and the best trainers, and not even enjoying any of it.

Wayne said Oak Hill was a full-service barn. That meant that these girls didn't groom, wash, or clean their horses. They didn't tack up or untack. When they went to a show, their horses met them there.

I'd had no idea. I'd thought show riders were just cleaner than the rest of us. I'd thought they got up to braid at four o'clock in the morning. I thought they had some magical way of cleaning tack that only took them two seconds. I never imagined that they had an army of grooms doing everything for them.

I wondered how people got this rich. Did they work harder? Were they smarter? I knew some poor people who worked hard as hell. I also knew some poor people who didn't. Some were sharp and some were dumb as dirt. But now I wanted to know where all this money came from and what you had to do to get it. We learned in history class about England and France and how if you were born a shoemaker or a factory worker there, then, by God, that was what you were, no matter how much money you made. Not only that, but your kids would stay in that class and so would their kids. But this was America, and it wasn't supposed to work that way.

Wayne took me to my car and I drove home. As I walked

across the porch, I could hear Donald talking on the phone, and I stopped to listen. He was talking to Melinda about moving, about all of us living somewhere else. He was telling her that his cousin in Bakersfield, California, worked in an oil refinery and could get him a job.

My heart jumped into my throat. I wondered if I should let them know I'd heard. I just wanted to scream. There was a trash bag on the porch that was about to split open. My father never would have left garbage on the porch like that. He would have taken it out to the trash can and then scrubbed the can in the kitchen clean. I pictured us out in Bakersfield, California, with the trash blowing across the porch.

The sugar maple branch scraped against the porch roof. There wouldn't be sugar maples there, either. What if he made us go before the leaves turned and came down?

I loved it best when the leaves came off that sugar maple tree, all except a little cluster on the east side. That tree had been the only thing blocking us from the Hardee's parking lot until Jimmy planted a cluster of white pines. Now you could hear people in the parking lot at night, but you didn't have to look at them.

I stood on the porch and looked in through the window. Donald pulled out a cigarette from his front pocket, put it between his lips.

I walked in the door. He knew I'd heard.

"My cousin said he can get me a job for seventy-five thousand with my management experience. Full benefits. Your mother knows and she wants to go too."

I pictured Melinda trying to grow tomato plants in the dry sand of California behind a sad little house that looked out on an oil refinery. She would die. I would die.

He was holding a silver lighter.

"That's my father's."

"Your mother told me I could use it."

"Well, you can't."

"Honey, your daddy is gone," Donald said. "I don't mean to be hard or nothing, but get over it."

"My father would kill you with his bare hands for saying that in this house. You are a no-good, lying son of a bitch, and one of these days Melinda's going to figure it out."

Damned if he didn't smack me right across the face.

I fell backwards onto the floor. I couldn't get up — I couldn't even breathe. No one had ever hit me before. I looked at his dirty socks and waited to see if he would come closer.

"I'm fourteen years old."

It just came out. I was so scared, I thought he might kill me.

He got so close to my face that I could see his yellow teeth, his red gums receding and showing their bare roots.

"See what you made me do with that mouth of yours?

Somebody's going to really hurt you one day for talking like that. And it might be me."

I crawled away from him and stood up, rubbing my face to make the pain stop. The way he was looking at me was weird, like he wasn't finished.

"Give me the lighter," I said.

He took a long drag, started to put the lighter back in his pocket. I grabbed for it, but he held it away. I smelled the smoke and liquor on his breath.

"What about asking nicely," Donald said.

"May I have that lighter?" I asked.

I was scared he was going to hit me again, and he knew it. He handed it to me but held on as I touched it.

"You need to learn to act like a lady."

I pulled the lighter away from him and walked out, wondering if he was going to chase me.

"Where you going? You can't take that car nowhere but to school and the barn!" he yelled.

I got into my car, locked the doors, and peeled out.

I couldn't tell Wayne what had happened or all hell would break loose. As tough as Wayne was, Donald was crazy. All the guns in the world were no match for crazy.

Before Donald, my mother and I had been planning to have a good life together, just the two of us. We were going to go to the beach. I slept in her bed for two weeks after Jimmy died, and we talked about all of it. She told me that she'd always wanted to go to Scotland where some of our ancestors were from and that we could go on an overnight trail ride together. But my mother was a captive now, and none of that was ever going to happen.

ELEVEN

Driving up Route 220, I decided I needed a gun. That bastard wasn't done with me. Jimmy would want me to get a damn pistol and put a slug right between Donald's eyes if he ever laid a hand on me again. That I knew for sure.

I saw the Tastee-Freez and pulled into the parking lot. Four teenagers sat on the hood of a car, laughing and flirting. I pulled some crumpled bills out of my pocket and picked a few quarters off the dirty floor mat, then ordered a cheeseburger and fries from the takeout window. I recognized one of the kids as the cute boy from the lunchroom. The other boy was his ugly, dimwitted friend. His family lived in the trailer park and fought with everyone in town about everything. He'd been in trouble for hunting on posted land, drunk driving, and selling pot, but he finally got his when he tried to lie to a game warden about his fishing license. In Allegheny County, that was like treason. The game warden took one look at his gap-toothed lying smile, arrested him, and sent him to jail for two weeks.

The dimwit looked me up and down. "Hey, ain't your uncle Wayne Stewart?"

I ignored him.

"'Scuse me!" he said, louder.

"Yeah, what if he is?" I answered.

"Does he live in that old shit shack down in the hollow?"

His girlfriend laughed.

I got ketchup for my fries, trying to ignore them. I was so hungry that I was shaking. I walked toward my car clutching the bag of food.

"I'm just asking," he continued. "Didn't think anyone could live in a house that had a hole in the roof. Does he have a toilet, or does he shit in the field with the donkeys?"

I faced him. The girls snickered.

"Come on, Tommy, stop it," said the cute boy.

I walked up to the dimwit, stopped, clenched my fist, and punched him in the mouth.

One girl screamed. The other one laughed. "Oh, Tommy, you got hit by a girl!"

"Keep talking about my family," I said as he grabbed his face. "I'll knock your goddamn teeth out."

Blood running down his lip, he grabbed me by the throat with both hands. "I'd knock you flat, 'cept I don't hit girls."

He tightened his grip until I choked, then let go. I pushed him away and got into my car, coughing.

"Poor white trash!" his girlfriend yelled at me.

"You oughta know!" I yelled back.

I drove half a mile and pulled into the entrance of the National Forest, shoving the food in my mouth without even tasting it. When I parked, I saw two kids making out in the back of a pickup truck. They saw me and sat up quickly, and I realized that it was Eileen Cleek and some boy from school. I put the car in reverse and drove away. Even Eileen Cleek, the girl everyone called a lesbo, had a boyfriend.

I drove up the mountain for half an hour, looking for June. He always made me feel better, but he wasn't easy to find. He only came out when he was walking to town to get his usual staples: cheese nabs, Dr Pepper, cornmeal, and kerosene. I wondered what it was like to live in the hollow with your brother and sister for seventy years, no electricity or running water. He always seemed happy, and it didn't take much to make him smile. I had only seen his sister, Maybelle, and his brother, Clifford, once, when I was ten. They had come to church for revival week. I'd never seen their little farm. Jimmy had told me all about it, but he'd always gone there alone.

I parked by the ram, hoping for June. The ram was an old pump the Army Corps of Engineers had put near Natural Well, and it made a low, rhythmic sound as it pumped cold water out of the ground and over the mossy rocks in the shade. This was near the path June took to get to his house, but no one else knew.

Boy, I bet they'd made some moonshine back in that hollow years ago. Wayne had explained to me how perfect these mountains were for homemade liquor — you got the clean water, the kind of trees that didn't give off much smoke, and the privacy of the deep dark hollows. Wayne and Jimmy used to get jars of apple brandy from somewhere up in here, but hell if I knew where.

I watched the ram pumping water, imagining it was corn liquor trickling through the rocks. I wondered how many people had sat here and thought the same thing. I waited, but all I saw was a big tom turkey fly along the fence line and nearly crash into a utility pole.

When it started getting dark half an hour later, I gave up and drove to Wayne's house. He made me a bowl of stew and handed me a blanket.

"What's the matter, girl?" he asked.

I shook my head.

"It can't be all that bad."

"Mind your own goddamn business," I said. "I don't want to talk about it." But then I started crying real hard. Wayne came over and hugged me. His arms were bony, but when he hugged me tight I could feel how strong he was.

"Donald wants to move out to the desert in California," I

said. It hurt more saying it out loud because it made it true. "I know Melinda will do it."

"Well, that's about the dumbest thing I ever heard. No Criser has lived or ever will live out in the damn desert."

"He wants to work at some oil refinery where his cousin works."

I could see a flash of worry deep in Wayne's eyes that he quickly covered up. The light from the television flickered across his face.

If we moved to the desert, I would never see Uncle Wayne again. The thought of it made me want to die. I wanted to ask him if I could live with him if that happened, but I was scared he would say no again. I was scared he would tell me he couldn't have no little girl living with him, that I would have to go with Melinda.

But I decided to speak up anyway. "Wayne, if they leave, I can't go there." I choked up again.

He looked at me like a statue. Then he crossed his feet in front of the fire.

"You can stay in the barn. But that donkey might stomp you while you're sleeping." He winked. "Of course you can stay here."

He threw another pillow to me, and I tucked it under my head and fell asleep. I dared anyone to come get me here at Uncle Wayne's.

TWELVE

THE NEXT MORNING, the sun was bright. It was the first day of September, and the air was clear. I told Wayne I didn't want to go to school.

"I'll bush hog the paddock," I volunteered. "Got enough weeds in there to choke an elephant."

"I ain't leavin' you here to run the damn rotary cutter all by yourself."

I made myself go to school, staying far away from the rednecks and skipping lunch entirely. I didn't tell Ruthie about any of it, how Donald had hit me or that I'd punched Tommy and he'd grabbed me. It would scare her half to death, and she would ask too many questions.

Ms. Cash talked about *As I Lay Dying*. Her eyes twinkled, and I knew she loved the book. I had read it, and most of the time I didn't know what the hell was happening, but I liked not knowing. I liked understanding something without having to think about it.

Most of the kids didn't get it, and they complained and

said it was dumb because the story was told with different people's perspectives. Why couldn't the writer pick his main character? Just when you understood one, the point of view changed to someone else.

"Maybe there is no real story. Maybe everyone has a different version, and they're all a little true and they're all a little false, and we should respect how everyone else thinks," one boy said.

Several kids nodded in agreement.

"God's version is the true version," said a girl. "The writer should try to think in terms of God's perspective."

I laughed out loud.

Some kids said it was a desecration when the mother's body fell out of the coffin. Poor Ms. Cash, trying to save their souls from the preacher who told them they weren't supposed to study anything but scripture.

I rode to the barn with Wayne after school, and the trip seemed shorter this time. Wayne told me about Dee Dee, how she was a champion rider but had a reputation for what he called "funny stuff." He meant that she gave her horses drugs.

I had read that people like that were always staying one step ahead of USEF—the United States Equestrian Federation—but sometimes their horses were drug tested at shows. One time, a lady's horse got disqualified after she'd given him a can of Coke and he'd tested positive for caffeine. Wayne didn't judge people who played around with the rules unless they were downright inhumane. So for him to make a comment about Dee Dee — that was something.

I looked for Wes but he wasn't around. Not like I really cared — I just thought I might run into him. I saw myself in the dirty tack-room mirror, my hair frizzy from sweating, circles under my eyes. Kelly had such smooth, shiny hair, and she was so confident.

I sat silently in the lunchroom while Uncle Wayne talked horses with the stable hands. I was picking at a blister on the inside of my knuckle at the base of my index finger.

"Let me see your hand," Wayne said. I showed him my palms, rubbed raw with fat blisters. He reached up into a cabinet, opened a saltshaker, and set it down. He opened his pocketknife and grabbed my hand. I jerked it away.

"Fine. It'll be infected and hurt a hell of a lot more than it does now."

I let him slice the blister open and rub salt into it. It burned like hell. I clamped my teeth down and my eyes teared up.

"After a few days, you won't need no gloves."

Wayne let me bathe a bay mare in the wash stall. I scrubbed her tail with soap and sprayed it with ShowSheen to repel the dust. I painted her feet with hoof polish, the dark lacquer dripping off the golden brush, leaving mahogany horseshoe prints on the concrete. I could have done it for hours. The mare liked me and closed her eyes sleepily while I worked on her tail. She rested her big head in the crossties and fell asleep.

I knew I could untangle this horse's dirty tail every day, clean her stall and a hundred more, wash every damn horse in the field, if I didn't have to speak to another human being for the rest of my life. Horses trusted me, and I could be myself around them.

Kelly, Wes, and Dee Dee appeared just as the mare pawed to get out, raking her metal shoe against the concrete, the grinding sound echoing through the barn. When Wes saw me, he smiled and said hello.

"Is someone watching this horse?" Kelly yelled. She sure didn't miss an opportunity to make somebody look bad. I didn't answer. I unhooked the mare from the crossties and walked her down the aisle.

It was time for Kelly's lesson, and there was activity in the barn. A couple of other riders were getting their horses ready to join her. Her mother was walking down the aisle inspecting horses with her arms crossed.

I saw a silver Mercedes pull into the driveway and park right next to the building. The driver was an old man who wore an oxford shirt and riding breeches with socks pulled up over them to his knees, worn loafers, and a tweed newsboy cap. His face was pink with gin blossoms. He opened his door, and a pint of vodka, stuffed behind old maps and mail, fell out from the door's side compartment and clinked on the gravel.

"Jesus Christ, Herbert," said the old lady in the passenger's seat. She had short gray hair and pink lipstick. *These must be the Wakefields,* I thought.

"No one saw, Martha," the man hissed.

He picked up the flask and tucked it into the door compartment. Two fat Jack Russell terriers spilled out of the car and trotted toward the barn.

"Grandma's here," Kelly called out to her mother.

I tied the mare to a pole and went back to the wash stall to get the fly spray. The Jack Russells trotted down the aisle as I returned. All of the horses ignored them, except one.

The mare saw the terriers and braced her front feet out, flared her nostrils until they were big round circles, snorted deep into her chest, and panicked.

"Whoa, mare!" I said, putting my hand on her flank and patting her to calm her down. I could feel disaster coming.

Wes had jogged in from the riding ring. Everyone in the barn — stable hands, Wes, Kelly, and Wayne — yelled, "Whoa!" as the mare ripped the metal bar out of the barn wall and took off full throttle toward the road. The jagged bar dragged behind her and whipped around her feet. Dee Dee came running out of the office cussing a blue streak. I was so scared the mare was going to kill herself that I almost passed out. I ran after her, praying she would stop before she got to the road or got tangled up and broke her leg. I slipped and fell into a gully covered in long grass and looked up to see Wayne grabbing the mare by the halter.

"Come here, you fool!" he told her. He unhooked the lead rope, and the metal bar fell to the ground. He turned to me. "Not a scratch on her. You're lucky."

I scrambled out of the ditch. Wayne walked the horse back to the barn, and she snorted at the terriers scratching their fat bellies in the aisle.

I tried to sneak into the tack room before anyone saw me, but Herbert and Martha stood there in their sunglasses staring at me.

"Well, my word!" said Martha.

"Good Lord," said Herbert, looking at the horse, then at me.

I tried to explain. "I tied her in a slipknot, but she was sitting back on the rope so hard I couldn't pull it loose —"

"The horse just got off the plane from Brussels. I'm sure they don't do 'slipknots' there," snapped Dee Dee. My mouth went dry and I started to sweat. "Who *are* you?" she asked.

Wes looked away — embarrassed for me, I guess.

"Dee Dee, shut up," said Martha.

"Fine, Mother. Let the horse run down Route 220 and get hit by a tractor-trailer."

Kelly was staring at me like she wanted to rip my head off.

"Are you new?" Martha asked me.

I didn't know which of them to talk to. They seemed like a bunch of witches, each one meaner than the last one.

"She's my niece. She's been breaking horses for me since she was a kid," said Wayne.

Kelly rolled her eyes. I opened my mouth, but I felt Wayne's hand clamp onto my shoulder. "I'll talk to Sid about how we do things around here," he said.

"Good idea," Martha said sharply.

Wayne nodded at me to follow him into the lunchroom. Spanish music was playing on the radio and a bunch of grooms were sitting around eating. I was so nervous, I opened my bag lunch and ate half my sandwich before I realized it was somebody else's.

"That'd been my horse, I woulda beat the tar out of him for ripping the barn apart," said Wayne. "You know why they're upset? 'Cause they paid a gazillion dollars for a horse that's afraid of a Jack Russell terrier."

"What did I do wrong?" I asked.

He lowered his voice. "Nothing. Not a damn thing. A slipknot is the safest way to tie a horse. But they like to put these hotheaded horses in breakaway crossties."

"But I couldn't get the slipknot to come undone when she panicked — "

"Because the bar broke. Ain't your fault." He unscrewed the top of his Pepsi and cussed loudly as it sprayed all over the floor.

I knew he was telling me the truth.

"You put Big John on the blacksmith list? He got a loose shoe in the back," he said to one of the grooms. Thank God they were talking about something else.

The door to the lunchroom opened, and Dutch walked in. I held my breath.

"I could fire you for that," he said.

I wanted to tell him that if the horse was afraid of little dogs, someone ought to work on that, since every barn in the world had at least one terrier scratching around. Wayne glared at me.

"I'm sorry, Dutch," I said. It was the most insincere apology in the world, and I was looking him right in the eye when I said it.

Dutch stared at me, blinking his eyes, sizing me up. Maybe he saw something familiar. I could tell by his face that he knew I wasn't sorry.

"We're short a groom for the show this weekend. Are you available?"

Edgar had walked in behind Dutch. He motioned for me to say yes.

I was surprised and didn't know what to say. Of course I

was "available." Did I want to work with these snobs anymore? No. But we needed the money, and grooming would be easy.

"Sure," I said.

"Be here at four a.m. Saturday. Sharp. You're working for Kelly."

He left.

"Why would they put me with Kelly?" I asked Wayne.

"Well, now, that's a good question," he said. "Maybe he's trying to teach you both a lesson. They'll pay you seventy-five dollars."

That could cover the electric bill and maybe the water bill, too.

"You'll work from four a.m. until after dark," said Edgar.

"Don't that violate some labor law?" I asked.

Wayne snorted. Edgar laughed so hard, he started coughing. "Honey, there ain't no union here," said Wayne, his white dentures gleaming as he laughed.

I worked and went to school the rest of the week, tired and bored. The calluses on my hands got tough, and I could feel myself losing weight. My T-shirt hung off my shoulders, and I had to wear a belt with my jeans so they wouldn't fall down.

THIRTEEN

SATURDAY MORNING, BEFORE dawn, I got out of my car at the barn, alone. My eyes burned from not sleeping. I was hungry, and the coffee I'd bought at the truck stop in Raphine was burning a hole in my stomach. I'd slept at home, not speaking to Melinda or Donald, passing them like a ship in the night.

It was pitch-black. Some of the grooms were washing horses and bantering in Spanish. Others loaded the show trailers with hay, straw, horse blankets, shiny tack, unmarked bottles, and every kind of leg wrap and bandage I'd ever seen. They hosed down the tires and polished the stainless steel around the wheel wells. I couldn't understand them, and they didn't speak to me much. But they did smile when they saw me, and I knew one thing: they would tell Wayne everything I did, right and wrong.

I walked down the aisle of the barn and heard the loud crunch of dozens of horses eating grain.

"Let's go!" a groom yelled to me. "Get in the back of the

blue rig. Ride next to Otter — he don't haul so good." He handed me a syringe with a bright yellow cap. "Here's a shot of ace, but only for an emergency. It's not legal for a show horse."

Ace is a tranquilizer. I put it in my jacket pocket and climbed into the back of the idling tractor-trailer.

"How long's the ride?" I asked the groom.

"An hour," he said.

He slammed the door, and I found myself under the heads of two horses kicking and stomping loudly. The truck pulled away from the barn with a jerk, and I braced myself with both arms.

One horse reached out and clamped his teeth down on the soft flesh under my arm, and I yelled, trapped between the two of them.

"Get off me, you son of a bitch!"

It felt like my arm had been slammed in a door. I elbowed him in the nose and he let go, staring down at me with the whites of his eyes showing. I cursed a blue streak and rubbed the mark, hoping nothing worse would happen to me back there.

I pulled out the syringe, took off the cap, and got ready to stab him right in the neck with it. I found that little triangle by the shoulder where you give a horse an intramuscular shot. But wait — which horse was Otter? I realized I was stuck next to more than a ton of horse, and the best thing to do was nothing. The other horse grabbed my sleeve in his teeth and pulled. I let him nod up and down, shaking my arm like a rag doll, until the sleeve of my coat was covered in slobber. As I steadied myself, the big rig heaved onto the interstate and powered up into a loud roar. The horse let go of my sleeve and played with the clip holding the hay net.

The sun was coming up when we arrived at the show grounds in Culpeper. The big rig parked, and I helped the grooms back the horses down the ramp one at a time. I walked them out in the freshly clipped grass and wiped off the white lather that had formed on their flanks and chests. I held each horse's lead shank while the grooms unwrapped their shipping boots.

I'd been to shows before, but not at this level. The horses I saw at the show grounds amazed me: barrel-chested hunters, springy jumpers, and Welsh ponies that were clipped and braided to within an inch of their lives. The riders schooling their horses at this hour were real athletes — all business, no chatter. I was surprised to see kids already in their show clothes working their horses over fences under the lights before the sun was fully up. The horses' foggy breath came out in bursts with each canter stride, and the coaches sat wrapped in their jackets with their hot coffee. It was only the beginning of September, but fall had come. Shadows were sharpening and the sun seemed low in the sky.

The riders were all dressed exactly — and I mean

exactly — the same. Their breeches all fit the same, with a little wrinkle in the seat, the crotch, and the knees, but not too much. Not too much stretch, either, but enough. They all wore the same brand of tall black field boots, the same short steel spurs with black spur leathers, the same navy coats and helmets. The tailoring and color of their clothing was so identical that if they'd lined up and walked in the same direction, they could have been an army parading in front of a review stand. I had pictures of riders in rust-colored breeches and charcoal pinstriped coats on my wall at home, but everyone here was dressed exactly the same and I didn't know why. It was intimidating.

I put the horses in their stalls in the tented barn that had been set up for the show. Then Edgar gave me a list of things to do. For two hours, I unpacked, raked the aisles, polished bits, and rubbed the horses down, looking over my shoulder for Kelly.

When I went to fill up water buckets, I found a moment to watch the first rider compete in the ring.

The loudspeaker crackled. "Number three hundred seventy-eight is on course. This is Czar, owned by Fairleigh Farms, shown by Eliza Niven," said the announcer.

A girl on a dainty chestnut hunter entered the ring at a working trot. They picked up a canter, made a large circle, and headed for a three-and-a-half-foot gate. The horse jumped it easily. I watched the horse transition smoothly after each fence, the rider's coattails fluttering open to reveal a charcoal satin lining as she looked up for the next one. I listened to the girl's mother at the rail. "Steady. Collect him. Sit up. Sit *up* . . . One . . . two . . . three . . . and . . . good . . ." The mother counted strides between fences, then turned away, trying to keep a poker face, muttering something about how the girl needed to concentrate.

I walked back to the barn, past lanky riders in their expensive show clothes. Their chin straps hung down unfastened. One ate a bacon, egg, and cheese sandwich while she sat in a golf cart with her feet propped up. Another slumped on her pony while a groom attached her spurs and her mother raced over with coffee.

In one of the warm-up rings, I saw Marshie Dunn, a well-known trainer. I had seen her only in magazines, and she was beautiful. She had smooth golden hair, cropped to her jaw line. She was coaching a boy on a pony back and forth over a vertical. Her voice was big, smooth, and reassuring, not sharp and dissatisfied like Dutch's. The rider was getting frustrated with the pony, so Marshie walked over to the boy and talked to him. She put her hand on his knee and smiled as she talked, letting out a big laugh as she rubbed the pony's face. I saw the boy sigh and relax. I could tell how much they all three liked one another — the boy, the pony, and Marshie — and I hoped they would win.

Then I saw Kelly cantering in another warm-up ring.

"Kelly, you are such a natural!" another rider said to her.

Anyone is a natural with a hundred-and-fifty-thousand-dollar horse, an army of grooms, and one of the best trainers in the country, I thought.

"Where were you?" Kelly asked when she saw me.

"Looking for you," I lied.

"Can you pick out his hooves?" she asked in a high, tight voice. "And keep his stall clean." She turned back to the other rider. "So . . . I want to sell him by the time I go to college and buy something new."

"You could go for something a little more pushbutton. He's kind of green, Kelly," the other rider said.

"Totally. I'm so over it."

I could not imagine calling a horse like that "green." He could have taken a blind old lady around that course.

Kelly pointed her toe, indicating for me to clean her boots. I dug a rag into the creases around the ankles of her boots, removing the dust and grime.

"When you're done, please get me some french fries," she said.

"Sure."

"She's never done this before," Kelly said to her friend as I walked away.

I wondered what it would be like to think about horses, shows, college, and boys without worrying all the time about everything. I knew Kelly's mother made her miserable, and she knew I knew. So why did she have to do this routine of pretending she loved to ride, pretending I wasn't in on her secret? I was. She hated riding. If she'd ever liked anything about it, her mother had taken it away.

I got the fries and ate a few before I took them to Kelly.

"They were five dollars," I told her. She looked at me with her mouth slightly open, then said, "I don't keep money on me when I'm riding." She laughed, cutting a look at her friend. She ate some of the fries and handed them back to me. "You can eat the rest if you want," she said. I threw them in the trash can. I wasn't eating her leftovers.

I followed her to the ring. When she started trotting the horse, I noticed that he was tossing his head and fighting her, trying to get his tongue over the bit.

"I think you need a different bit," I called.

Kelly looked at me like I was crazy. I knew I would get yelled at for this, but I was right, and I decided I didn't care what she said to me. It wasn't fair to the horse.

"He hates that bit. Try a plain snaffle," I said, digging myself in deeper.

"We always ride him in this. He's just excited to be here." Kelly smirked.

"Well, he's sticking his tongue out like a dog."

"No, he isn't," she said.

"Yes. Look."

She pulled his head around so she could see his big tongue hanging out, and then she walked him over to me.

"If you don't like it, we'll switch back," I said.

"Fine," she said under her breath.

"Good idea." I turned and saw Wes. "I'll get it," he said.

Wes jogged back to the barn and returned with a plain snaffle bit. They took the bridle off the horse's head and switched the bits. Kelly trotted the horse again, and this time he dropped his head.

I looked at Wes and he winked.

"Sid, you can go back to the barn," Kelly said.

I went to the tack room and wiped down saddles by myself, but I couldn't stop smiling.

FOURTEEN

THAT AFTERNOON, KELLY got second place in the Maclay class, meaning she had ten points toward the twenty-five she needed to qualify for the regional competition, which might lead to the nationals at Madison Square Garden. I waited for her to thank me when she came out of the ring with the silver plate and ribbon, but instead she snapped at me in front of everyone for letting the horse eat grass with the bit still in his mouth.

Before dark, Kelly left the show grounds with her mother while Wes and the grooms worked. I hoped Wes would offer me a ride, and I imagined what we would talk about. But when I looked up, I saw him pulling away in his truck, alone.

I looked down at my jeans. They were covered with hoof polish, which would never come out. I was sunburned. I had hay in my hair and a ring of sawdust in the cuffs of my pants. How long had I been walking around looking like this? Angel, one of the grooms, was putting shipping boots on one of the ponies. He was about as spit-shined as you could get.

His towel was neatly folded and resting on his shoulder. His jeans were clean. His hands and his face didn't have a speck of dirt on them. Angel must have read my mind, because he came up and brushed the sawdust off my shins with his towel.

I rode back to the barn with the same two horses, and by the time I got there, my legs were shaking from standing up so long. I was exhausted. When Wayne saw me, he just laughed. He was putting down a deep blanket of pine shavings in a horse's stall. It was late, and I wondered why he was still there.

"Wait until you see the horse coming here tonight," Dutch said to us.

"It better be the Baby Jesus himself, with all this fuss," said Wayne as he fluffed the shavings. I rubbed Bag Balm onto my cracked hands.

Blinding headlights cut across the center of the barn. I heard the growl of a big rig and the hiss of its brake releasing. The truck pulled up next to the barn, and the driver cut the engine.

Dutch walked toward the rig, a jog in his step. He grabbed a lead shank with a chain from a tack trunk and motioned for Wayne to join him. The driver hopped down and told Dutch the horse had vanned well. Wayne and Dutch pulled down the back door.

I saw the horse's rump back carefully down the ramp.

He was black or black bay and wore a white cotton shipping blanket. Shiny buckles connected the surcingles holding it across his chest. Wayne guided the horse down, his hand on the horse's hip, and the horse stepped onto the pea gravel. He let out his breath, picked his head up, and sniffed the air.

Wayne looked at the horse and let out a long whistle. The horse was spectacular.

"This, my friends, is Idle Dice," Dutch said.

I walked closer. "*The* Idle Dice?" I asked.

"*The* Idle Dice."

"Why is he here?"

"Martha Wakefield bought a controlling stake before he was injured."

He was syndicated—owned by a group. Most syndicated horses are stallions. If he was syndicated as a gelding, that was because he was a top-level performance horse. A big earner.

Idle Dice turned and looked right through them. Then he looked me in the eye, and I felt a chill.

"Let him stretch his legs. He's been on that rig since Atlanta," said Dutch.

Wayne led Idle Dice to the indoor ring, and the horse sniffed the ground loudly. Other horses called to him, and Idle Dice called back from deep in his chest.

"He sprained his back, so we're going to rehab him," Dutch said.

Wayne removed his leg wraps and shipping blanket, unhooked him, and let him go. The horse trotted away from them, shaking his head, happy to be loose.

"He's something, ain't he?" said Wayne.

"I'd like to see him with someone on him, see how bad his back is," said Dutch. "I'll get Kelly on him in the morning."

"It don't look so bad to me," said Wayne.

"That's what I was thinking," said Dutch. "I could just get on, but I want to see him from the ground."

"Put Sid on," said Wayne.

Dutch laughed, but I knew Wayne was serious. I could tell by his voice.

"I'm telling you, put her on."

I glanced at Dutch but his expression hadn't changed. Maybe he was ignoring us.

I cleared my throat, which felt like a vise. "My saddle's in the car," I said.

"We'll wait until tomorrow and have Kelly ride him," said Dutch. "He just got off the trailer."

The horse walked by and snorted at us. With little effort, his strides ate up the ground underneath him. His neck was so long that he reminded me of a dinosaur. The bones in his face were fine and chiseled, but his nose was square, almost Roman, and his eyes were big and dark.

"She's been riding since she was two years old," growled Wayne, "and by God, I'd put her on anything."

Dutch, irritated, turned to look at Wayne. All three of us wanted to see this horse under saddle tonight. What if there was nothing wrong with him? What if the vet was wrong? It happened all the time. But there was no good reason to put just anyone on Idle Dice immediately. It was unsafe, bad training, and bad horsemanship.

Dutch looked Wayne in the eye.

"You promise she can really ride?" he asked.

Wayne thumped the fence impatiently with his hand.

"Fine — put her on. But don't tell anybody I did this."

"Do I have to wear a helmet?" I asked.

"Just get on the horse," Wayne said through his teeth.

We tacked him up. As Dutch gave me a leg up, the horse hopped excitedly. I hung on as Wayne tried to hold him by the reins, but the horse took off across the ring. I got control and let him canter and toss his head. The horse was so responsive that I simply closed my fingers around the reins and he turned. He dropped his head, tugged lightly on my hands, and let me know he was happy to get to work. I felt like I'd stepped out of a go-cart and into a fighter jet.

"He's got a little hitch in the back. I think it's in his right hip," I said.

I saw Dutch nod.

"It gets better as he goes. Maybe he just needs some exercise," I said as I circled close to them.

Wayne leaned up against the fence, chewing on a piece of straw, with a twinkle in his eye and a creeping smile.

Suddenly, I heard a familiar voice.

"Interesting decision, Dutch, putting a stable hand on his back when he's just gotten off the trailer. That horse was worth more than two million dollars before he injured himself."

It was Martha, in her Barbour coat and tennis shoes.

"I thought . . ." stammered Dutch.

"You thought I wasn't coming tonight," she said.

She studied me carefully.

"I will say, she is a nice rider," she said, as if I weren't there.

"Yes, she is," said Dutch. I wondered if he was just being agreeable, but it sure was nice to hear, either way.

"That's something you don't see so much anymore. She's giving that horse room to do what he wants. I wish Kelly would ride more like that, rather than being such a showoff."

They all watched me without speaking. I loved it.

"I think he has a tight right hip, not a sprained back," Martha said. "We'll start working him tomorrow and take him to the show next Saturday."

"Next weekend?" asked Dutch.

"This horse loves to show. It'll make him happy," Martha said.

"Kelly is already riding two horses that day."

"Then this girl," said Martha.

"Sid?" asked Dutch.

"They're a good match. Why not?"

I brought the horse over to the rail.

"What do you think?" Martha asked me sternly.

"I think he's pretty cool," I said. "He's got so much power, but he's also just . . . really sweet."

I gave the horse a hard pat on the neck.

"He likes you," Martha said.

"You're riding him at the show next weekend," said Dutch, his mouth barely moving.

I studied their faces and saw that it was true. I felt like I was dreaming. I had always wanted to ride a horse like this, and I had started to think it was never going to happen.

Wayne leaned back farther on the fence, holding the piece of hay in his teeth, and looked up at me.

"Better shine your boots," he said.

FIFTEEN

MARTHA TOLD ME I had to take a lesson with Dutch, and he scheduled it for Monday afternoon. I was kind of nervous. I put on a nice polo shirt that actually fit and tucked it into my jeans with a leather belt. I found a suede brush in the trunk of my car, hidden in the candy wrappers and old assignment sheets that had never made it into the house, and I brushed my gray chaps until they were smooth. I found Idle Dice's bridle in the tack room, rich brown Hermès leather with raised white stitching and a shiny double-reined pelham bit. I pulled my hair into a tight ponytail, tucked it into my helmet, and took my saddle and the bridle to Idle Dice's stall. When I walked around behind him to attach the girth, he stepped aside like a gentleman, then stepped back once I was done. What a professional.

I wondered where he had learned his manners, and I realized it was from his grooms. They had to be the ones who'd taken the time and effort to teach him. Ladies like Martha

Wakefield would have fed him treats until he was so spoiled and rude that you couldn't get near him.

When I got home Saturday night, I was so excited that I burst through the door looking for my mother. Usually I would know better. Usually my mother would roll her eyes, or shake her head, or interrupt me, but I knew this time would be different. Melinda knew horses, and she wanted me to do well and make money, didn't she? I had finally gotten a foothold, and Melinda would think of how badly Jimmy would have wanted it. She would help make this happen mainly because she was my mother and she loved me.

"Who's paying the entry fees?" she'd asked.

"She is. Mrs. Wakefield."

"You ain't a charity case."

"I know that. I'm doing her a favor."

"She thinks you're a poor kid who needs a handout."

Melinda's eyes were dark and scary. She looked so angry that I took a step backwards. I felt my chest tighten. It was horrible, to go from feeling so good to feeling so pathetic in a couple of seconds.

"The horse world is a club for rich people, and the sooner you realize that you're not invited, the better."

I went to my room and closed the door. The pain started to subside, just a little, when I realized that, as usual, I didn't need her help.

∪ ∪ ∪

I walked Idle Dice out to the mounting block. His shoes clinked slowly against the asphalt, so much time between strides because he was such a long, lanky horse. A couple of the grooms stopped and looked, and one of them took the reins for me and held him by the block while I mounted up. Idle Dice was one of those horses who could not and would not stand still while the rider got on — polite as he was, he was impatient and wanted to get to work.

"I do not give lessons to riders in chaps," a voice boomed, shattering my happy moment and sending me into a panic before I had even gotten into the ring. I turned to see Dutch walking out to us with his clipboard, cell phone, and coffee, his fat Welsh corgi trailing behind and looking right and left to steer clear of oncoming hooves.

"Excuse me?" I said.

"We wear boots and breeches because that's what we show in. This is not a warm-up or a hack. It's a *for-mal les-son.*"

I felt small and scared, and my arms, which were usually strong, were mushy like noodles. I wondered whether he was trying to scare me. "I don't have show boots — "

"Find some today, and some buff breeches. Not cream, or gray, or navy, or rust. Buff. Seventy-three percent cotton. You can buy them online at Dover. I need to see what you will *look like in the ring!*" he shouted.

I looked at him out of the corner of my eye. He was

adjusting one of the fences, pulling out the metal pin and sliding the jumps to make them higher. I had a lump in my throat.

"I don't know where you got that hat, but you need a USEF regulation helmet."

A USEF regulation helmet cost hundreds of dollars.

Dutch looked toward the barn, where Kelly was coming out on another horse.

"Sid — posting trot. Kelly, collect that horse. Wake him up before you get in here." He grabbed a crop and threw it to Kelly, who caught it and gave the horse a smack behind the saddle.

I gave Idle Dice some leg, and he launched into a powerful, springy trot. I sat up and adjusted the reins as he curled his chin toward his chest and played with the bit.

"Don't let him get behind the bit," Dutch barked. "He's a smart horse — he thinks he can do it by himself. Don't put him on cruise control."

The whole lesson was like this. Dutch set up little cavaletti jumps for me, so small that Idle Dice cantered right over them like he was insulted. Dutch yelled at me about my weight not being in my heels, my back being round, my wrists being floppy. He made me trot at him head-on and said my right toe was sticking out too far. The list went on and on. Could we at least jump a real jump? It wasn't going to happen. He made me trot around without stirrups for so long that I got sick to my stomach from the pain.

Then, when my legs were shaking, I was soaked with sweat, and I could feel the skin on my shins rubbed raw and oozing, Dutch started setting up a course. A real course. Airy verticals and huge oxers, at least three feet three inches high. He set up the deepest jump in the deepest part of the sand, where it would be hard for us to get up and over it. These fences had bright, glaring colors, rainbows and stripes among the fake stones and brick. I didn't know too many horses who would walk by them without balking, let alone jump over them. My palms started sweating.

"Sid, pick up a canter. Red coop." He pointed at the red-painted wooden box with front and back sides slanting toward a pole at the top, like the roof on a chicken coop. His voice was loud, monotonous, detached. It was scary.

Idle Dice, hearing the sound of Dutch's voice, started to jog in place. He chewed on the bit and walked sideways like he was performing in the dressage ring. He knew the sound of a coach preparing a rider for a course.

I simply opened my fingers a quarter of an inch and the horse launched into a big canter.

"Easy. You have a lot of stride," said Dutch.

I had never heard these terms before. Wayne would just say, "Whoa."

I brought Idle Dice deep into the corner and looked up at the coop, locked on to it like I'd seen the Olympic riders do, and let my body turn to catch up with my head. I focused on the jump like a laser.

"Soften," said Dutch, meaning I looked a little tense. The horse would start to feel my resistance and harden up, go faster, and not respond as well.

"Don't lean into the turn. You're not riding a motorcycle. Now oxer, vertical, vertical, stone wall."

I looked at the other fences. No time to size them up or let Idle Dice see them.

We cantered up to the first fence, and I could feel the horse adjust his stride and hold his breath when he left the ground. When he landed, he exhaled and continued. Same thing for the oxer, then the verticals. He knew to steady himself for the oxers, which were deeper, so he wouldn't pull a rail. He knew he could use more speed for the verticals, which were only about a foot deep. The horse seemed to know that I was making the decisions, and he responded with respect to everything I wanted. I loved this horse.

"Great," said Dutch. I felt relieved to hear a nice word. "But your equitation needs work, kid. Shorten your stirrups a couple of holes and get your heels up under your hips. I want to see a proper crest release. Welcome to the twenty-first century."

I had been using an automatic release all my life, like

the old-time classic hunter riders — I let the horse's mouth pull my hands as he jumped, following the motion with my hands, keeping contact. I'd always thought it was better, but I knew it was harder.

"Sometimes harder isn't better," said Dutch, reading my mind. "The advantage to a crest release is that you maintain better contact and you don't have to regain it as you're landing. An automatic release can encourage the horse to be too forward, and then you have to take a couple of seconds to collect him. In a big equitation class, you don't have a few seconds. You have to land preparing for the next fence."

He put his hands on my foot and took it out of the stirrup, showing me where my toes needed to be. He grabbed my calf and I winced from the saddle sores. Seeing my reaction, he unzipped my chaps up to my knee, saw the raw spot on my leg, and made a face.

"Put some Desitin on that and wear tall boots next time. You're not riding in your backyard anymore."

We did the course five more times. Dutch told me that I was on a horse with an enormous stride, so to fit five strides in between two of the fences might be too hard — maybe we should just do it in four. We tried both ways. One time, I thought too hard and stiffened up, and the horse chipped in — crammed half a stride in before the jump — and it was ugly. It looked like he'd shuffled or even stumbled. If a horse like this chipped in, it was entirely the rider's fault. Dutch explained that I was counting when I should have been using my eye, but I didn't understand. I'd always used my eye, but the more I thought about the strides, the worse it got. I remembered Kelly having this problem, too. Finally, Dutch told me to let the horse find his takeoff spot before the jump, and he did.

Afterward, I saw Kelly in the barn when we were both washing off our horses. I thought about walking around to the other door and avoiding her, but I walked past her instead. She looked me up and down, as usual, while she let her horse drink out of the hose.

SIXTEEN

"ANYBODY CAN BE clean and neat and dress well regardless of his financial position," George Morris wrote in *Hunter Seat Equitation.* I read this for the hundredth time in Wayne's truck on the way to the tack shop in Charlottesville. It might have been true, but I didn't see how I could look like other girls at the show. Those clothes were expensive. If you wore a hand-me-down, you looked like a fool. I took a deep breath and kept reading.

> Jackets, both for summer and winter, should be attractive yet conventional and, most important of all, fit well; there is nothing more detrimental to a rider's posture than a loose, baggy coat. . . . Breeches should be of any tan, gray, or canary material.

Every pair of breeches cost at least a hundred dollars, and they had to fit. I'd have to buy an old pair and have them taken in, but wouldn't this be obvious? Would they be clean? It would be so easy if I just had the money.

> As far as boots are concerned, make sure that they are tall enough to give the rider as much length of leg as possible and fit snugly in the calves. I prefer any black or darkish tan boot (a field boot is nice), preferably without tops.

There were gorgeous used field boots — tall black leather boots with laces on the front of the ankle — at tack shops everywhere. But they would stand out. All the riders wore new boots. Did I want the judges to notice me because of my riding or because I was wearing a pair of thirty-year-old Vogel boots? I could read between the lines — George Morris seemed to be telling me to find some boots that would get the job done, that I didn't need to wear exactly what everyone else was wearing. He even said "preferably without tops" — the tops were only for the hunt field — but he would allow it if you needed to do it. He would allow the girl who spent her Sunday mornings in the hunt field to wear the same pair of boots to the show. *What a sacrifice . . .*

> All in all, a rider entering a show ring should appear elegant in an understated, conventional way.

> No part of his riding attire should draw attention to itself and under no circumstances should there be any flashiness. Imagination can enter in subtly tailoring clothing to the rider's build and in coordinating colors with the horse.

In other words, *don't stand out*. Back to the nine-hundred-dollar boots, so I wouldn't draw attention to myself.

Wayne waited in the truck while I went inside. I had the seventy-five dollars I'd earned grooming for Kelly and my first paycheck, which wasn't much. I'd decided Donald could pay the electric bill himself if he wanted the lights on.

I found the kind of helmet Kelly had been wearing and the boots the girls had at the show.

Yep, three fifty for the helmet, which wasn't even a GPA, and nine hundred for the boots. I went to the used rack, but the prices were only half off. I left.

Wayne saw my face and said, "Borrow something from the barn. It's just one show. Don't matter what color it is, don't have to be too fancy."

"Have you been to a show?" I asked him. "They are all dressed exactly the same. They all have the same Ariat Monaco field boots that cost nine hundred dollars."

"Dumbest thing I ever heard! You need a pair of black or brown tall boots, period!" he shouted.

"I'm not standing out like a sore thumb with brown dress boots!" I said.

"Then borrow some from somebody at the barn."

"I don't want to ask some rich girl if I can borrow her boots! They're custom fit, anyway."

We dropped the subject. Wayne popped in his old Osborne Brothers cassette tape and we listened to it all the way home, not saying a word.

The next day, not one of my days at the barn, I thought maybe thirty times about how I was going to get show clothes. When I got home from school, I called the barn and asked to speak to Edgar.

"I need some boots. Please don't tell me I can wear some old used dress boots that don't fit—"

"No, you need to wear what everyone else is wearing," he said in his deep voice.

"Thank you!" I nearly yelled into the phone.

"Wayne doesn't get it. You cannot stand out. People will know you are new, and they will be asking who you are. You must be dressed exactly like every other rider. I'll find you a helmet and some boots. They might not be perfect, but they'll be fine for one show."

"You understand."

He laughed. "This is what I do."

"I'm supposed to have another lesson with Dutch this week."

"You don't have to. I'll tell him the horse is tired. Just come out and hack him around the ring."

"Are you sure?"

"Yes," he said confidently.

It dawned on me that Edgar ran everything. Dutch, Dee Dee, and Martha thought they called the shots, but they didn't. Edgar just let them think they did.

When I got to the barn the next day, Edgar handed me a helmet. It was a little beat-up and too small, leaving a red mark on my forehead. But whatever. Now we had to find boots.

"Kelly has an extra pair," he said. "You could ask her."

"No way," I answered.

He found an old pair of boots that belonged to a boy who didn't ride there anymore. The calves were very tight and the feet were too big, but when Edgar shined them up, they looked good. If only I didn't feel like my legs were in a tourniquet. Edgar also found a riding coat, breeches, and a shirt, and he would have them sent out to the cleaners for me, but just this one time.

The sleeves of the coat were too short, but he showed me how to tuck in my cuff so it wouldn't be so noticeable. The breeches were too tight in the waist, so I safety-pinned them.

The shirt was old and had someone else's monogram on the collar, but the coat would hide it.

"Go straight to the horse show grounds on Saturday," Edgar said. He smiled big. "This weekend, you're full service."

SEVENTEEN

On Saturday, Wayne drove me to the show grounds in Keswick. I walked to the tented barn area where grooms were playing loud salsa music. Idle Dice was being braided by a woman I'd never seen before. A professional braider, I realized. With a braided mane, Idle Dice's neck looked enormous, and his plaited forelock tucked up tight between his ears made his huge eyes look even bigger. As he chewed, muscles filled the hollow sockets above his eyes. His coat was so black and shiny that it looked purple.

While I was standing there, a groom came along with Idle Dice's tack, entered his stall, and put it all on without looking at me. He pulled the horse out into the aisle, wiped off the sides of his bit, pulled the hay out of his mouth. When I reached out for the reins, he looked at me strangely and walked the horse to the mounting block, motioning for me to follow. Then he took a walkie-talkie off his belt and said into it, "Idle Dice is ready and heading to the ring."

Now I really got it. This was how girls on the A-circuit

stayed clean and relaxed, not exhausted or dirty. They had grooms. They had someone to clean the stalls and wrap the legs, braid, feed, water, polish, and scrub. They didn't touch hoof polish when they were dressed and ready. They didn't clean out the grime from between a mare's udders or the snot from a horse's nose. They didn't pick the scabs out of a horse's ears from fly bites or put salve over the wounds to heal them.

How was this fair? How could you say you rode horses — and won horse shows — if you'd never had to do these things? Maybe there was a trial period, and once you graduated, you just got a groom and moved up. Maybe it was my turn to move up, and I would never have to dig to the bottom of a filthy stall again.

But I knew this wasn't true. These girls were just lucky. I thought about Wayne and what kind of rider he would have been with a setup like this. It wasn't fair — at all.

"Spit-shined and ready to go!" I turned around and saw Wes. I was so happy to see him that I didn't know what to say.

He reached under my chin strap and tucked my hair up.

Edgar was watching. "You don't have a hairnet? Wait here." He jogged over to the next aisle, rummaged around, and came back with hair spray and a hairnet. He took my helmet off, fixed my hair, put a net over it, sprayed it, and put the helmet back on my head.

"Ahh, much better," said Wes.

"Just like the other girls," said Edgar. He winked.

I took Idle Dice into the warm-up ring, where trainers and riders were crammed together, going in every direction. We weren't all the way in when I almost collided with a girl. She said sharply, "Heads up, please," like I was some kind of idiot.

Dutch walked into the center of the ring sipping his coffee, but he was chatting with another trainer and didn't look at me. I couldn't figure out the traffic pattern, so I just got in behind some girl on a blood bay and picked up a trot. Girls were coming off jumps kind of fast and then merging with other horses at a trot, going both directions. No one was walking. But I just kept following the blood bay, trying to get into a pace. My legs were getting numb because my boots were so tight. My back was stiff and my helmet itched.

I saw a trainer in the center of the ring staring at me, arms crossed. He was dressed in fancy dark jeans and an insulated vest, and he had a sour look on his face. He leaned over to another trainer, an older lady with short hair, and whispered something, still looking at me. I wished I knew what they were saying. As I came around the ring the first time, I heard a lady on the rail say, "Is that Idle Dice?"

"Sure looks like him," said the woman next to her.

"What is he doing here?"

"I don't know."

"Who is that on him?"

"I have no idea."

It was quiet in the warm-up ring, even though there were at least twenty horses and about eight coaches all standing together in the center where the jumps were. The fancy flooring in the ring — it looked like mulch but wasn't — absorbed all the sound. All I could hear was the jingle of the chain of a pelham bit and one roarer — a horse that had a wheeze.

I saw Wayne walking toward the rail with his hands in his pockets. I waited to hear what he had to say.

"Eyes up" was all he said.

So, with people staring at me and whispering, with Wayne not saying much, with Dutch not paying attention, I decided to get out from behind that blood bay horse. It looked like the faster horses were closer to the center, and they were merging with the horses coming off the jumps. So I picked up a big canter and moved toward the center. Idle Dice had such a big stride that he ate up the ring faster than all the others, and they moved out of my way. What a nice canter he had, like a rocking horse. It was impossible to look bad on him.

Suddenly, Kelly came out to the ring, ducked under the rail, and made a beeline for Dutch. Dee Dee was right on her tail, jabbering. Kelly was ignoring her. She was gesturing and upset, pointing to her eye. They all stopped and looked over at me. I wondered what on earth they could want with me at this point.

Dutch raised his hand and gestured for me to go over to them.

"Sid, Kelly's horse scratched his cornea. He can't show."

"Oh, that's too bad," I said.

Kelly threw up her hands as if to say, "Hello, why do you not get this?"

Dutch went on. "She's trying to qualify for Maclay, so she needs to ride Idle Dice today. Sorry about that."

I was stunned and didn't say anything. I looked over to see Edgar holding Kelly's saddle. He came into the ring. Kelly fastened her chin strap.

"Sid, you can get off," Dee Dee said.

I was so upset, I was shaking.

Kelly took the horse's reins under his chin and I dismounted, not because I understood what was going on — I was still in shock — but because people were starting to look. Edgar took my saddle off and handed it to me. He seemed angry but wouldn't look me in the eye. They put Kelly's saddle on, and she mounted up and patted Idle Dice's neck, talking baby talk to him. She gathered up the reins and walked into the crowd of horses schooling, and that was that.

I carried my saddle out of the ring to Wayne.

"What the devil is going on?"

"What does it look like?" I said. "Kelly just found her new equitation horse."

We watched the show from the grandstands.

When the Maclay equitation class came up, we looked for Kelly. She had Idle Dice too tight.

"Why is she all up in his mouth?" I asked.

Wayne just shook his head. He looked really sad, and it made me feel horrible. Seeing him so disappointed nearly tore my heart out. I hadn't realized until that moment how much he wanted this for me.

Dutch started actively coaching from the rail. I strained to hear what he was saying. "Soften. Soften. Open your hands." He was trying to be calm but he was getting emphatic. Dee Dee was right there, looking as tight as bark on a tree.

Even though Kelly was tense and hanging on his mouth, Idle Dice managed to put in a beautiful round, and Kelly got first place. Ten more points toward the regionals. One more good equitation class would do it.

Wayne and I rode home in silence.

Finally, as we were coming down the mountain, he spoke. "The right thing for me to do is to tell you that this ain't for you, that you don't have the money. If I had a conscience, I'd do that. But I don't have a conscience. So I'm going to tell you that if you work hard enough, you can beat her."

"I don't care," I said.

"That's a lie and you know it. You'd like to grind her into the dirt. You're a better rider than she is."

We pulled into my driveway and he turned the motor off.

"Listen, kid. Once you ride a horse like that, there ain't no going back."

I got out and went inside. I could hear his truck leave.

No one was home. I went into my room and shut the door. I looked at the posters all over the wall, of the U.S. Equestrian Team, of George Morris, of the puissance classes in England where the horses jumped seven-foot walls. I lay down on my bed and closed my eyes to sleep, but I started to cry instead.

The next morning I got up first thing and drove to Wayne's. I felt awful and I wanted to talk to him. I knew he would have recovered from the disappointment and would have something tough and clear to say about all of it. He would make me laugh and help me get my head screwed on the way it should be.

But when I walked inside his house, I found him sitting on his bed, drinking a beer. He looked up at me. "I don't get a day off?"

"You're drunk," I said.

"Half-drunk."

He shifted his weight and there was a loud clunk that made me jump. He reached under the bed and pulled out his .44 magnum, a big silver pistol with a long barrel.

"Good Lord," I said. "Are you Yosemite Sam or what?"

I reached out to touch it and he handed it to me carefully, barrel down.

"It's loaded?" I said.

"Of course it's loaded. Why the hell anyone would have a gun in the house that isn't loaded is beyond me."

I pretended to tuck it into an invisible belt and then whipped it out, cowboy style, pointing it at the wall.

He laughed. He knew I could handle a gun. Wayne, Jimmy, and I had spent many afternoons shooting bottles off a log with Wayne's old single-shot Winchester rifle.

"Can I take this home?" I asked.

"What for?"

"'Cause Donald has one in his truck, and Melinda doesn't have one at all. Do you really think Donald should be the only one with a gun?"

"Take it home but don't say anything. And don't shoot yourself by accident."

I put it on his bureau and stared at it. Just looking at it made me feel better.

"Don't you tell him you got it. Hear?"

I nodded.

Wayne went to the kitchen and opened another beer. It was only seven thirty in the morning.

When I got home, I tucked the pistol under my bedsprings. I felt like someone had been in my room, looking through my things. Melinda would never do that.

I heard Donald talking on the phone, and I realized he didn't know I was there.

"I know, Mr. Sheffield, I'm sorry. I thought . . ." Someone on the other end was yelling at him. "I know, sir, I'm sorry. I'll be there tonight and I'll work a double shift, and I'm sorry." The man yelled again and hung up. Donald cursed and grumbled to himself. I hid in my room without making a sound, scared as hell he was going to find me, until he left.

EIGHTEEN

MONDAY MORNING I stopped by Ruthie's house to pick her up for school. I drove up the dirt driveway and honked as her daddy was coming out in his work clothes, ready to go to the mill. He waved to me and walked over to say hi. I loved Earl. He had this big head and big smile, meaty cheeks, and a dimple in his chin.

"Mornin', girl. You up all night doing that history paper?"

"Yeah," I lied.

"You girls are too smart to stay around here all your lives. You'll wind up working in the mill, like me." He grinned.

Why did people always say this?

"I don't think I could work in the mill," I said.

"That's what I used to say." He chuckled and tapped on the roof of my car, then walked to his truck. "You girls mind your manners and do your homework."

Ruthie and her sister, Dorine, who was eleven and went to junior high, came out and got into the car.

"Does your daddy know I don't really have my learner's permit?" I asked her.

"No. But now he will 'cause of Dorine's big mouth."

"I won't say nothing," Dorine said. "Damn, Sid, I thought you was fifteen."

"I'm almost fifteen. Who's counting, anyway?"

"Why are you so grumpy?"

I guess I looked as worn out as I felt. "I'd like to tie a couple of sandbags to Donald's ankles and shove him over the Gathright Dam, for one."

"Just shoot him and tell God he died," Dorine said.

"It's tempting."

"I'll be damned if I'd let some lady sleep over at our house and start bossing us around," Dorine went on.

Ruthie's mouth fell open at the thought.

"Can you imagine that?" I asked Ruthie.

"No. You put it like that and I can't," she said.

"I'd kill her myself," Dorine said.

Ruthie turned around and stared at her sister. "Dorine, I better not be fishing you out of juvenile hall in a couple of years."

"Did Ruthie tell you she's applying to a private school?" Dorine asked me.

Ruthie looked horrified. "See what I mean about a big mouth? Nobody has any privacy."

"A what?" I asked. "A private school? Where?" She'd been hiding something from me.

Ruthie glared at Dorine. "I'm applying to the Madeira School up near Washington, because that old bitch guidance counselor is making me."

"What do you mean, she's making you?" I asked. Ruthie was bullshitting me and we all knew it.

"I couldn't afford to go there anyway," she said.

"You can get financial aid! You got a single dad who don't make no money," said Dorine.

"Dorine, shut up!"

We rode along in silence, me considering what it would be like if Ruthie left. I wished I'd never gotten out of bed.

NINETEEN

THE NEXT COUPLE of days, I went to school and then to Wayne's afterward. He was drunk the whole time. I felt like I should be there so the house didn't burn down. I did my homework, or at least some of it, in his living room while he snored on the couch. I called the barn and told Edgar that Wayne was sick, so he had someone cover for us.

I drove to the barn myself one day after school. If I'd gotten caught on the interstate, I would've been in trouble.

I was cleaning stalls when Martha sneaked up on me. I nearly jumped out of my skin.

"Would you like to show Idle Dice this weekend?"

"No thanks."

"Kelly is showing a horse we're trying to sell."

"Which classes?" I asked.

"Something easy," Martha said.

I wasn't sure why she said that — easy for me or easy for Idle Dice. "I thought you said Idle Dice likes a challenge."

"Well . . ." Martha hesitated.

"You don't think I'm ready for an equitation class?" I asked. I must have been losing my mind, talking to her like that. But I figured I might get to show Idle Dice only once, and I wanted to make the most of it.

"It's really hard," Kelly said, walking over to us from the wash stall.

"Jumping ten fences is really hard?" I asked.

She sighed. "Sid, it's not just ten fences — it's broken lines, and weird distances, and the jumps are three six."

"I've been setting up courses like that since I was nine years old," I said.

I was talking too much, but I couldn't stop. Kelly was making me mad as hell and I wanted to make her sorry.

Martha shrugged. "You can take him in an equitation class."

"Which one?" Kelly was obviously upset.

"Maclay," I said, upping the ante as far as it would go.

"You want to take him in a Maclay class at an A-rated show," Kelly said, laughing. She looked at her grandmother for help.

"Then do it," Martha said. "But you need more polish, and I want you to research some old Maclay courses online so you know what you're getting into."

She turned to Kelly. "Loan Sid your old boots, and help her find a better jacket."

As soon as they were out of earshot, I tried to call Wayne. His phone rang and rang, but he never picked up.

A truck pulled up behind the barn with a load of pine shavings and dumped it out, spilling everything into the parking lot. While Edgar and I were shoveling it into the shavings stall, I told him what had just happened. He raised his eyebrows and smiled.

"How does Maclay qualification actually work?" I asked him. "Not that I'm going to place in this class, but if I did, what would happen?" I had never paid attention to the technical part.

"There are Maclay equitation classes all over the country," he said. "You need to compete and place in a certain number of classes to go to the regionals, and then you need to place at a certain level to go to the finals. If you compete in a zone with a lot of other riders, you need to place higher in the classes to get more points."

I was already lost.

"What are the classes, exactly? Just a tough course? How do you qualify?" Maybe I should have asked these questions before I said I wanted to do it.

"Hang on," he said, and he went to the tack room. He came back with a piece of paper and we ducked into the shed to look at it. He'd ripped it right off the tack room wall. I read: "All contestants are required to perform over at least eight fences at three six with or without wings. To be judged on seat, hands, guidance and control of the horse." There was a complicated point system based on how many riders there were and where they placed.

I realized I was holding my breath. "How many kids make it to the finals?"

"Two hundred," he said.

"How many are competing in Maclay classes all over the country?"

"Thousands. Go straight home and tell your uncle. I can send in your registration to Maclay so that if you place this time, you get points. Who knows — on a horse like that, you could make it to the regionals."

I just stared at him, wondering if he was kidding, and he took the pitchfork out of my hands. I jumped into my car without taking off my coveralls.

The police on the Allegheny side of North Mountain never go over the top of the mountain, and the police on the Rockbridge side don't, either, so for a while I was in a no-man's land. As I was coming down the mountain, I was going about eighty, and as soon as I crossed out of the free zone, I hit radar and a sheriff's department car came shooting up from a service road behind me.

When I pulled over, the deputy asked to see my license. He was Barry Sitlington, who'd just graduated from my high school. I looked like a filthy gingerbread man in those

Carhartt coveralls, my hair still had shavings in it, and I had dirt on my face. Looked like I had just escaped from a nut house, or maybe a chain gang.

"I don't have my learner's yet," I pleaded. "You know my daddy died, and I had to work for my mom, and I'm sorry — I will never do it again. I know I was going too fast."

He escorted me all the way to Covington and tipped his hat when I got off 64. He was kind of cute with that gap between his front teeth, but why the heck would anybody want to be a deputy?

I couldn't wait to tell Wayne I was going to get another chance to ride Idle Dice, and not just any chance — I was taking him in a Maclay class. A real Maclay equitation class, a qualifying class for Madison Square Garden. Not that I would place, but I would get around those ten fences if it killed me.

But when I got to his farm, Wayne was nowhere to be found. His truck was gone. I waited around for a while, and then I went home.

I called him that night and the next morning. I drove up there after school. He wasn't there, and he hadn't been back. Grittlebones was there and meowing for food. No water, either. I dug around in the mudroom until I found a bag of cat food. I knew it! Wayne didn't want anyone to know he'd bought food for a cat. I gave Grittlebones some food and water and scratched his head.

I saw that the horses hadn't been fed that day, threw two bales of hay out into the field, and broke them up. The white bathtub had only about six inches of water in it, so I filled it. I didn't know where the hell Wayne was, but I was worried. I wrote him a note and left it on his door.

> I hope you're alive. If you are, you might want to let me know, and you might want to feed your horses, because I ain't driving over the mountain to do it every day. I'm riding Idle Dice in the Maclay class at the Charlottesville Horse Show on Saturday morning.
>
> Sidney

TWENTY

On Saturday morning, I woke up at dawn and drove straight to the show in Charlottesville. I was so worried about being pulled over, I drove under the speed limit the whole way. I figured I'd be lucky if I didn't wind up in jail before I got my learner's.

Edgar was there when I drove in. He gave me Kelly's boots and a navy pinstriped coat that fit me nicely. He made me take off my hat and try again to pull my hair into a ponytail and flip it up into my helmet.

Wes brought me some coffee and a roll, and he hugged me hello, for good luck, I guess. I never thought about boys, or kissing, or anything like that, but if I did, it would have been right then. He smelled kind of sweaty, and like soap, and I could see that his brown eyes actually had green in them. He had big hands and short, filed fingernails. When he adjusted my helmet, I froze like a scared rabbit, and I was glad when it was over.

When the judges posted the course for the Maclay class,

everyone flocked over to see it. I kept looking around for Wayne. Dutch walked the course with all the other trainers and riders. I followed him, but he only talked to Kelly.

The course looked kind of hard, with a weird coop coming off a corner. A lot of horses might shy at that one. Where was Wayne?

"What are you looking for?" It was Edgar.

"My uncle."

He looked away, like he might know. "I've got to help Kelly in this class. Do you need anything?"

"I don't know what I need. Let me ask you one thing—does this horse have a stop in him?"

I pointed out the weird jump on the course. I had to know if the horse would refuse a jump like that.

He chuckled. "This horse won't stop at that fence." He shook his head. "Ever."

They posted the order, and there I was, tenth out of twenty-two. Kelly was first.

I watched her in the warm-up ring. Her mare was hot—jogging in place, pulling, shying.

"Did you lunge her?" asked Dee Dee.

"Yes," Kelly answered.

Dee Dee leaned in toward Dutch trying not to be overheard but I heard her say, "Dutch, we don't have time for Kelly to ride her down."

I saw Dutch whisper to Kelly. She dismounted and they walked the mare back to the barn. I heard Kelly say to Dee Dee, "He's going to give her a little something."

"Where are they going?" I asked Edgar when he walked by. I wanted to hear it from him, but he didn't acknowledge my question. He looked angry and defeated.

"Edgar?" I said, louder. He glanced at me. "What are they doing?"

"I have no idea," he said. I could tell he didn't approve, and that was why Dutch was doing it himself.

Edgar saw the outraged look on my face. "You focus on *you*. Understand?"

I didn't answer. They were going to shoot the mare up with something to make her seem more calm, then sell her to some poor fool. My respect for Dutch evaporated. Did that mean I should disregard everything he said?

"It's confusing," I said.

"Dutch is a great trainer — he knows what he's doing. But he wants to win too much." Edgar ran his hand down the bridge of Idle Dice's nose. "Look who you get to show today. I think you're the one with the advantage." He smiled.

I walked Idle Dice around the show grounds, waiting for the class to start.

A little something.

Kelly came back with her horse and put in a beautiful

round to applause and Dutch's loud whoops at the in-gate. The mare was cool, relaxed, totally different. I wondered what they'd given her.

I stared at the course until I knew it forwards and backwards. The ring starter was going through the list the way they always do after every round. "Jamie, then Kaitlin, then Emma, then Morgan, then Liza, then Eleanor, then Catherine." And finally, my name was called. My hands were sweating, my heart was pounding, I was about to hyperventilate. We went into the ring, just me and Idle Dice.

We picked up a canter and he clicked into gear. He took each fence like a pro, but his stride was big, so I really had to work on keeping him collected. When I pulled back on his mouth, it didn't help. I had to both sit up straight and relax. I took deep breaths and pretended, when I breathed in, that the air was going all the way down into my feet, the way Wayne had taught me. I thought about him saying, "Just get in there and do the course. Stop worrying."

Idle Dice collected his stride. When we came around the corner to that spooky fence, I worried that he might stop, so I gave him leg, and he charged up to it nearly at a gallop. "Whoa!" I said, pulling him back as we landed, then turning one hundred and eighty degrees and doing the outside line, oxer to oxer.

Phew! We were done. I patted Idle Dice's neck and trotted him out of the ring.

The first person I saw was Martha. "You galloped up to that vertical."

"I was afraid he wouldn't go over it."

"This horse will not refuse a jump. You could have pulled the rail."

I knew she was right, but I really didn't care. I'd just completed a Maclay course.

I hopped off the horse, rolled up my stirrups, and tried to give the horse to Edgar, but he stopped me.

I watched the other riders go, sizing up each one. They were all more polished than I was, but all of them made mistakes. It would be up to the judges which errors were forgivable and which would push the rider out of the ribbons. I had no idea if I would place, and I braced myself for the worst.

"Please jog your horses in the following order. Ninety-five . . . One hundred fifty-one . . . Eighty-nine . . . One hundred twelve . . ." said the announcer.

I'd won the class.

Speechless, I jogged Idle Dice into the ring to accept my ribbon.

The ribbon was the deepest, darkest blue I had ever seen, like the wings of an indigo butterfly. It was the most beautiful thing anyone had ever given me. I kept touching the white centerpiece and running my fingers over the gold letters on the ribbon itself. All ribbons are beautiful, and I'd gotten a few of them at the local Bath County and Goshen shows, but

I had nothing like this one. The streamers were long, and I folded them gently in my hand the way I'd seen the top riders do.

I patted Idle Dice while he chewed on the bit. The horse knew we'd won. There was no doubt. His ears had shot forward when I jogged him into the ring, and he'd beamed.

Then there was a flurry of people talking around me. Martha was smiling but still complaining that I rode too forward. Kelly was patting Idle Dice and baby-talking to him.

"You just got thirty points. You qualified for the regionals!" a lady said to me.

"Thirty points?" I asked. I had only been thinking about getting through this trip.

"You're very lucky — this year it's right close by, in Warrenton. Last year it was in Kentucky."

"This is my first Maclay class," I said.

"Wow! Then you better take this horse to the regionals."

Wayne came down from the stands, half-drunk and red-faced. I didn't know what to say to him. I felt as though he'd abandoned me. He looked at me through all the booze and I could see his eyes were welling up with tears. He couldn't even speak, he was so overcome. We both wished he was sober.

"How long have you been here?"

"I saw your round," he said.

Wes jogged over to congratulate me. "Beautiful!" he said.

"I get to go to the regionals!" I said to him.

"I know!" His smile faded, just a little. "But you got a problem. Kelly just qualified, too. She's riding Idle Dice in the regionals, so you'll need to find a horse."

Right on cue, a groom came and took Idle Dice back to the barn.

"You want some lunch?" Wes asked.

"No thanks," I said.

He patted my arm. "You'll just have to find something to ride."

I stood there with Wayne, my helmet still on, and we watched Idle Dice leave.

Edgar came over and congratulated me, and then we all just stood there, the three of us. There I was, holding my blue ribbon, horsehair on my pants, and no horse to ride.

Kelly was squealing and jumping up and down with her friends from the barn.

"I think Dutch shot Kelly's mare up with something before the class," I said to Wayne.

"I don't doubt it," he said.

Edgar looked away as though he didn't want to talk about it.

"What happens if USEF comes and tests horses?" I asked.

"I've been to hundreds of shows, and I've seen USEF about three times," Edgar said.

I turned to Wayne, who was leaning on the fence.

"What am I going to ride? I have two weeks."

"You really want to do this?" Wayne asked.

"Yes!"

He looked at Edgar. "Beezie," he said.

"Yep," said Edgar. "Beezie."

TWENTY-ONE

Beezie Winants. The crazy old horse lady Wayne used to date. Rich as Croesus and smoked like a chimney. Lived in a trailer in Craigsville. Bought horses at Keeneland every year, only got around to breaking half of them.

Wayne drove me to Beezie's place. A bunch of foxhounds stood on their hind legs in a pen howling as we got out. Wayne knocked on the trailer door and Beezie came to the window looking like an old ghoul. Then she saw him and smiled.

She had a lot of land, maybe eighty acres, and about twenty horses. Most of the horses were turned out full-time. They looked good, but there were about ten of them in each paddock, and they were biting and kicking each other. They had mud caked all over them.

She opened the door. She was wearing dirty wide-wale corduroy pants, rubber galoshes, and an old sweater. The trailer smelled like cat, and sure enough two black and whites came to the front door. One took a look at us and saluted with his back leg, licking his ass.

"You taking care of all these horses yourself?" Wayne asked.

"Hell no. I ain't that stupid," she answered, and she winked at him. "How are you, sweetie?"

"Well, I'm fine," he said.

"Want to come in and set for a spell?"

We went into her trailer, which was packed full of horse equipment, like she'd brought the barn into her living room. Buckets, brushes, a hose, a box of bits, and a stack of yokes and tracings from a carriage. She saw me checking out the tracings, which looked so pretty all wound up and oiled.

"You like to drive?"

"A little bit," I said.

"She can drive a team," Wayne said.

"I remember you, Sidney Criser, from when you were a little girl on that nasty pony, Little Bear."

I laughed. I had loved our crazy trail rides with that pony.

"Ornery little thing with no tail," she said.

She was right. Some kid had tied Little Bear's tail to a tree, and when he'd taken off, his tail had broken, so they amputated it. After that, he just had a little puff of horsehair in the back, so you had to carry a flywhisk when you rode him.

I wondered when Wayne was going to get down to business.

"You got any good ponies?" she asked. "I'm looking for a real broke Welsh pony. Medium or even large."

He laughed. "Ain't we all!"

"Well, you find one and I'll buy it from you."

"I'll keep that in mind."

Ask her, Wayne. Just ask her, I thought.

"You know, I lost that black gelding. He had toxemic colitis, I think," she said. "What a shame."

"I'm sorry to hear it," Wayne said.

"He was down and sick when I went out to feed. We got him in the trailer and took him to Staunton — couldn't get to Virginia Tech in time. He died before it got dark. Terrible diarrhea, all day."

"That's awful," I said. I hated stories like that.

"Yep. I was sad. Real sad. Those two Broaddus boys came over here to help me clean out the trailer — their mama sent them, I guess. They were being real loud and obnoxious, and my horse had just died, and I didn't want to hear it. They was carrying on, laughing, jumping around in the trailer, shooting each other with the hose. Finally I went out there and I said, 'You boys might want to be careful. The horse that was in there yesterday shit himself to death, and I wouldn't want to catch that disease if it was me.'"

We laughed.

"I thought it wasn't contagious," I said.

"No" — she laughed harder — "it's not. You should have

seen their faces! They about died of fright. They were scrubbing their whole bodies with Betadine!"

Ask her. Ask her, I thought.

"What are you doing, Sidney? You riding much?"

"She's helping me out over at Oak Hill," Wayne offered.

"Oh, really? How is old Dutch? He loosened up any? He's so tight, he squeaks when he walks."

This meant that she'd tried to sell him a horse and he'd either gotten her down too low or hadn't met her price. Being Beezie, she'd been trying to take Dutch to the cleaners, and he wasn't having it.

We were off the subject . . . again. If he didn't bring it up soon, I was going to do it for him.

"We need an equitation horse. Sid qualified for the Maclay Regionals," Wayne said. "She won a Maclay class on that jumper Idle Dice, Martha Wakefield's horse."

"Well, I'll be damned," Beezie said quietly, sitting back in her chair and nearly boring holes through my head with her blue eyes.

"I figure I should go to the regionals," I said.

She stared at me for what felt like a long, long time. "I went to the Medal Finals in 1975," she said.

"I didn't know that!"

She shot a look at Wayne.

"I told her — she just forgot," he lied.

"They're doing the Maclay Finals at the Garden this year. I saw it in the *Chronicle*," she said. "So tell me about old Martha and that horse, Idle Dice."

"I got to ride him in a show, and I decided to take him in an eq class, and we won. But now Martha's granddaughter is taking him to the regionals."

"What's that horse like?"

"Big stride. Totally broke."

"When you say 'broke,' how broke?"

"Pushbutton."

"Well, I don't have anything pushbutton," she said sternly.

"Sid can ride anything, Beezie," Wayne jumped in. "She just needs the closest thing you got to an eq horse."

"I got a gray mare who is broke and sweet, loves to jump, supple, gets all her leads, rocking-horse canter. Snaps her knees right up under her chin and turns on a dime. But she's got a stop in her."

A nightmare for an equitation rider.

"There's nothing you can do about it. She'll just decide to stop. All the schooling in the world hasn't broken her of this habit, so don't stay up all night trying to fix it. You'd just wear yourself out."

I knew this wouldn't work. I couldn't get all the way to a horse show and have the horse refuse a fence.

"But that's all I got."

"She sound?" Wayne asked.

"Of course she's sound. She trailers fine, cribs a little." Meaning she chewed on the fence while sucking air — cribbing is the horse version of biting your fingernails, except horses can practically chew a barn down, so they wear a cribbing strap around their necks to stop it. "She's a good girl. But she's got a stop. She might get around twenty courses without refusing, or she might slam on the brakes at your first fence. It's a genuine stop, not a dirty stop." She meant that the horse would stop because she was spooked, not because she was being dishonest and trying to throw the rider. "You could try to use her to qualify, but I wouldn't take her to the Garden. Might waste a lot of money that way."

I took a deep breath and looked at Wayne. "How much for a three-week lease?" he asked.

Beezie laughed. "I'll let you borrow her for free. Maybe Sidney could come over and ride some sale horses for me this winter."

"Sure," I said.

We went outside and walked over the hill on the gravel road. Beezie opened the metal gate and banged on a feed bucket. Three horses came walking over the hill, and I saw the mare. She was dapple gray, dark mane and tail, a nice expression. Sure enough, she started cribbing on the fence.

Her name was Ruby.

We went back with a trailer and picked her up that night.

U U U

I told Edgar what I was doing, and he found me a new helmet, boots, and a coat. I didn't know whose they were. The coat was too big, but it was the best we could do. The boots were my first Ariat Monaco's, and boy, were they nice. Soft black leather, hidden zipper up the back so I didn't have to use boot pulls to get them on or a bootjack to pull them off. The person they belonged to must have had one leg larger than the other, because the right one gaped open a little at the top and I had to keep hiking it up. But I didn't mind.

I got on Ruby the first day after school. I trotted her over poles — no problem — and then we cantered a vertical — fine — and then I turned to do an outside line of two oxers. I thought about her stop, and sure enough, she stopped. She slammed on the brakes so hard, I fell onto her neck and did a flip over her head, landing on my knees in the dirt.

"Well, there it is," said Wayne. I got up, tightened the girth, and got back on.

"Just over a plain old white oxer," I said. "Wait until she gets in the ring and there are kids and dogs and all kinds of shadows."

"Beezie said there wasn't no rhyme or reason," he said. "Here's what I think: I think you forget that horse has a stop and you just take your chances. If you get it in your hea that she might stop, she'll sense it and she'll stop. She can tell you're worried."

"She can't tell what I'm thinking."

"The hell she can't. You tell me: were you thinking about the stop when she stopped?"

"No."

"You're lying. I'm not saying the damn horse can read your mind, I'm saying you tense up just a tiny bit and it'll make her nervous. If she's one whisker nervous, she might stop. You look at that fence, and you think *jump!*"

I nodded.

"I wish Beezie had kept her big mouth shut about the stop," he said.

TWENTY-TWO

AT FOUR O'CLOCK on a Saturday morning, less than two weeks after we'd gotten her, we loaded up Ruby and trailered her three hours to Warrenton. When we got there, the grooms were unloading the Oak Hill horses.

I started braiding Ruby's mane and realized that it looked horrible. I'd braided a few times before, but I had never gotten good at it. Show braids were supposed to look perfectly uniform and tight. The braids I had done were too fat, the yarn was too pale, and little hairs were sticking out all over the place. Plus every braid was a different size. I had tried to do it just like it said in *Practical Horseman;* I had separated the mane into perfectly uniform sections and clipped each one with a hair clip. But the mane was slippery so I couldn't get hold of it and so thick that each section was less than an inch wide. I knew I'd be doing it all day.

Wayne thought braiding was ridiculous, and he was no help. Edgar looked at Ruby and told me two things: one, I shouldn't have washed her mane — they're easier to braid when they're dirty—and two, I shouldn't have put ShowSheen in it. I hated that silicone spray but thought I had to use it, since it repels dirt. He said you use it after the horse is braided, but not on the mane. So I rewashed Ruby and tried again. It still looked horrible.

The lady who braided for hire was standing on a stool the next aisle over, wearing a tool belt with yarn, scissors, thread, and needles and working on a horse. I asked her how much braiding cost. She said it was a hundred and twenty dollars, which I didn't have, for the mane and tail. Wayne looked at his watch, said I had two hours and hadn't even schooled the horse, and told me I was second in the order of fifty riders. The lady said she'd do it for eighty this time. Wayne pursed his lips and reached for his wallet, peeling off four twenties. I was so relieved that I wanted to hug him, but he was too annoyed. I took the lady to Ruby, and she pulled up her stool and got to work, her fingers moving so fast that I couldn't see what she was doing. She sewed up each braid with thread and a needle, like a surgeon.

"Braiding a doggone horse's mane and tail for eighty dollars. I'm in the wrong business," Wayne said. "This is the last time I ever pay for someone to braid your horse."

I almost died when I saw the course. It was an indoor arena, and it was small, with terrible lights. If Ruby ever stopped, she'd stop there. The standards on one of the jumps were big fake Sauer's vanilla extract bottles left over from the

Grand Prix class, sponsored by Sauer's. Wayne sucked on his dentures, walked around the ring a bunch of times. "I'm going to stand by that jump," he said, pointing at the bottles. "When you come around, I'll cluck if she needs it."

"As if that's going to make any difference. You heard Beezie — there's no rhyme or reason."

"Just listen to me," he said. "You go deep into that turn, and you collect her. You get her ass up under her, use a spur or leg or your stick — whatever. Get her collected and tight, ready to go."

Forty minutes later, I was on course, for real. The first six fences were great, and then I came off the coop and had to cut around hard to the crazy fence with the bottles by the end of the ring. Ruby wouldn't have time to look at it. I thought *jump* like Wayne had said, and I sat up. Then I felt the horse suck back and look at the fence with her ears up. She was thinking about stopping. Wayne was standing by the rail, waiting to see what would happen.

I growled under my breath, "Git up, you bitch!" and I dug my outside spur into her right side as hard as I could, since I knew that was the direction she'd run out. She swished her tail, angry, and she galloped to the jump so hard, she nearly tore one Sauer's bottle down. But she jumped it, and she didn't even rub a rail. When I came out of the ring, Wayne grinned.

We watched all the other riders go. I couldn't find too

many faults. One horse ran out and refused, a few rails were pulled here and there, another half a dozen or so were rubbed.

I had no idea how we'd done.

Wayne said he thought the judge had liked how I'd "cowboyed" Ruby over the jump. Some judges appreciated that, once in a while. He said they got tired of watching kids who were passengers instead of riders, and they wanted to see someone ride the damn horse, not just sit there and pose. That had never been a problem for me. Wayne thought I would place.

When it was over, they started reading our jog order, and they called me twentieth. Kelly placed fifth and was jumping up and down and shrieking. You had to get nineteeth or higher to qualify for the finals.

I'd missed it by one place.

TWENTY-THREE

I LIKED OLD RUBY. I rode her a few more times, and then we returned her to Beezie and I said goodbye. Beezie invited me to come ride again, and I knew I would.

It was the beginning of October, and it was really feeling like fall. I was already behind at school; I didn't feel too good about that. I had been reading the books Ms. Cash told me to read, but my midterm paper was late. She told me she wanted it done in two weeks or I was going to fail. I stayed up and wrote it in one night and then turned it in the next day.

I hadn't been speaking to Donald or Melinda at all. I was hardly ever home. One night when I was there, they called me into the living room and sat me down. Donald said he was planning to take that job in Bakersfield once it was official. My mother looked excited, and she let him do all the talking.

"Sidney, there are opportunities there for all of us," he said.

I laughed. "I ain't going to California," I said.

"You will if your mother tells you to. You're fourteen years old and you do as she says."

"I ain't going."

My mother looked upset. "I ain't leaving you here," she said.

Donald cut a look her way when she said this, and I realized that *he* wanted to leave me here but she wouldn't. Well, Christ Almighty — maybe she did have a backbone. Maybe I could get her to stay.

"You can't make me move to California," I told her.

"Where are you gonna live? Wayne's?"

"You're damn right," I said.

"I won't allow it," she said.

Donald stood up. "I'm taking that job, Melinda, so if you don't come with me, then you can just stay here by yourself."

"Would you let us sort this out?" she snapped.

"Don't you raise your voice at me."

"It would be nice if I could have a goddamn conversation with Sid without — "

He grabbed her by the arm and forced her backwards into the kitchen. She cried out, and I could tell it hurt.

"I sacrifice everything for you, and you sit here without a job doing nothing," Donald roared. "Not even raising your kid. You just take my money and sit on your ass. Don't you swear at me."

I thought about getting out that pistol and putting one

between his eyes right then and there. I'd count to ten, and if he hadn't let go of her, then that was that. When I got to seven, he let her go and walked out the front door.

I could hear her crying. I went into the kitchen, and she was standing there like a scared dog.

"Get that man out of our house," I said. I prayed, actually prayed, that she would say, "Yes, I know." I prayed to God in my head, *Please, please, please . . .*

But she didn't say anything. I stood there waiting for her to settle down so we could figure this out the way we used to figure things out.

Then she said this to me: "You're trying to ruin my life."

And I realized she was crazy.

In my car, driving up Route 220, knowing I might never sleep under the same roof as her again, I started crying so hard that I could barely see. I felt like my mother was dead.

I drove to the farm. Wayne was asleep, drunk, on the sofa with the TV on. I slept there and went to school in the morning, and at lunch I told Ruthie what had happened, all of it. She just sat there chewing her food, shaking her head. I figured she was probably on her way to a fancy boarding school anyway, so what did she care.

TWENTY-FOUR

After school, I went to the barn alone. I had stopped by Wayne's place on my way, but he stank of liquor so I left him home. I wasn't cleaning stalls half an hour before I heard Dutch chewing out Wes over some horse getting cut up in the field. Wes had been walking the perimeter of the field for more than an hour but couldn't find what had done it — a nail, a piece of metal, whatever.

To listen to this while I was thinking about my mother was too much. When Dutch finally left, I found Wes. "You don't have to let them treat you like trash."

He tried to ignore me. "Maybe they hired a pig farmer from Massies Mill because they knew he'd never stand up for himself. You'll be here until you're a tired old drunk."

"Don't be blowing your stack at *me,* Sid. I'm the only friend you got around here."

I climbed up to the hayloft and threw down a few bales, broke the bales into flakes, and hayed all the horses, working with one of the grooms. When I was done, Wes was standing in the aisle looking tired.

"You hungry?" he asked.

"Yeah."

"I'll drive."

I got in his truck and we drove over to White's, the local horsemen's hangout, home of the "Mammoth Burger." I'd only been in there once, with Wayne. Charlottesville was different from Covington — the cars were a lot nicer and the people had more money. There were terriers bouncing up and down in trucks in the parking lot and the people inside had on nicer coats than they would near my house, but you'd be surprised how much we all had in common. Horse people just wanted to talk about horses, gossip, make deals — you know, the same everywhere.

Wes acted like I hadn't said what I did. I couldn't believe I was sitting there with him. I felt like my life was in the damn toilet, yet suddenly it didn't seem to matter so much.

"I heard you almost qualified for the finals," he said.

"Yeah."

"That's incredible."

"Thanks."

We ordered cheeseburgers and fries.

"Even if someone gave me a horse for the show, I'd have

to pay for all the other fees," I said. "The board at the Garden, trailering, entry fees, the hotel room. That alone would be . . ."

"Six grand. Maybe more," he said.

"Shit. That's a lot worse than I thought. Even with a loaned horse?"

"You wouldn't get a free horse, Sid. If you went, you'd have to take something really broke, a real eq horse. And even if you borrowed one, you'd have to insure it."

I sat back in my seat and sighed. "Oh, well — doesn't matter because I didn't qualify." I kept looking into Wes's eyes. I felt as though he really understood and he cared.

He blinked and looked away. "Maybe next year," he said. But we both knew it had been a fluke and wouldn't happen again.

"How's Wayne?" he asked.

"Wayne's not doing too good right now."

Our food came pretty fast, and we ate for a few minutes. I changed the subject. "Who's your favorite horse in the barn?" I asked.

He smiled. "That fat old pony, Cherokee," he said.

"Out of all the expensive horses from Germany and Sweden and Saudi Arabia, he's your favorite?"

"You try him out sometime — you'll see. He'll jump anything. You'll rub your hands raw trying to hold him back. He's got to be eighteen years old, at least, and he bites kids.

But, man, is he fun to ride. You point him at a fence and he just takes off."

"So, you don't mind working for rich people?" I asked him.

"That's where the money is."

"How'd you get the job?"

"I was at a show once, working as a groom, and Kelly's horse colicked. They found him in the stall about to die. The vet was an hour away, so I ran a tube down his nose and pumped him full of mineral oil."

"All by yourself?"

"Yeah."

"Damn. That's one thing I can't do on my own," I said.

"The horse wasn't going to make it otherwise — I didn't have any choice. So they hired me because they wanted to keep someone with vet skills close by. I got accepted to a summer vet program at Virginia Tech, but the money at Oak Hill was too good, so I stayed."

I was impressed. "Virginia Tech is one of the best vet schools in the country."

"I've got a good gig. I'm lucky." He shrugged.

"I think they're the ones who are lucky."

I was kind of embarrassed after I said this.

"Thanks," he said.

The waitress brought the check. Wes grabbed it and pulled out his wallet. "My treat."

"Thanks," I said.

I wondered if this was a date. I sure wanted to think so.

We got in his truck and went back to the barn. Dutch was hauling a sale horse up to The Plains and no one was around, so we decided to go on a trail ride. I got to ride Cherokee. The second I got on his back and sank my weight down into my stirrups, he took off. I gathered up the reins while he was running through the parking lot.

Wes nearly fell over laughing. He climbed onto his gelding and threw his leg forward in front of the saddle to tighten the girth.

"I told you! I told you he was crazy! He loves trail rides," he said.

We trotted down the edge of the field and cut through the woods. Cherokee knew which way to go, so I got in front. You're only supposed to let a horse run when you're heading away from the barn — otherwise they get in the dangerous habit of taking off for the barn when you head home — so we skirted the edge of the field and let them tear. Cherokee was running so fast that tears streamed out of my eyes from the wind. We cut into the woods where Wes said there were some jumps set up. Cherokee tore down the trail and jumped over those coops and gates like they were nothing.

It was so damn fun to be on a horse with no one watching what you were doing, knowing the horse was going to go over the fence because he wanted to.

We walked home to let the horses catch their breath. I wanted to ask Wes about Kelly. I couldn't, for the life of me, figure out what he would want with her. But it didn't come up.

TWENTY-FIVE

When we got back to the barn, I heard Kelly in the tack room arguing with Dee Dee and crying.

"But she's my best friend!" Kelly said.

"I don't want you sharing a trainer with her anymore. Dutch gives her too much attention and it's going to cost you."

They were talking about Margaret, the girl I'd seen with Kelly on my first day. I knew she and Kelly were best friends. Margaret boarded her horse there.

Kelly begged her.

"It's always 'The Margaret Show,'" said Dee Dee. "She needs to find another trainer."

Dee Dee was making the girl leave a few weeks before the finals. Wow.

"She's pretending to be your friend but she just wants to beat you," Dee Dee said.

"She *is* my best friend." Kelly was still sobbing. "You're making her move Limestone? He loves it here!"

"I have to talk to the vet. I don't have time for this," Dee Dee said.

"You only have horses because you hate people," Kelly said as Dee Dee walked away. "And they hate you back."

I saw Dee Dee's face, and she was hurt. She saw me and tried to hide it. I wished I hadn't heard any of that. I didn't like either of them, but I felt bad for both of them. Kelly was right — Dee Dee liked horses more than she liked people. She had horses around because she was lonely.

Then I felt a cold shiver as I wondered if I rode horses because I was lonely, too.

Wes and I just stood there. Finally, Kelly came out of the tack room, saw us, and dried her face off on her sleeve. "Where've you been?"

"We just took a short ride," Wes said.

"Sid, you left Gee Gee's stall unlocked, and she got into the tack room and cut up her leg."

I felt the blood drain from my face. Immediately I assumed it was my fault. Then I realized that it wasn't — I hadn't been near Gee Gee's stall all day. Why did everyone blame me for everything? Did everyone hate me that much?

"The vet is sewing it up," she went on. "Twelve stitches."

Wes went to help.

"I wasn't in there," I said.

"Everyone knows you were. You were cleaning her stall this afternoon."

"I was not in there today. It must have been someone else."

"Like who?"

"Hell if I know."

"Well, we know it wasn't your uncle. He's sleeping under a bar somewhere."

That was it. I didn't care how upset she was — she wasn't going to insult my family.

"I have news for you, sweetheart," I said. "If I want to knock your teeth out, Wes ain't going to stop me."

"You're fired," she said. "If you want to get paid for the day, you better finish cleaning stalls."

"Screw you," I said.

"Just get out."

Everything was happening so fast, I didn't have time to think. I got my chaps and my saddle from the tack room and went outside.

As I loaded my tack into my car, a big silver Range Rover pulled into the driveway and a lady got out wearing jodhpurs and rubber boots. I recognized her as an official I'd seen at the horse shows. What in the hell was she doing here?

Martha came out to meet her.

"Hello, Madeline," she said.

"Good evening, Martha."

"Is everything okay? Is this a USEF business call?" Martha asked.

"Actually, it is. Your granddaughter is a beautiful rider. I'm so happy for her that she qualified for the finals."

God, it was so insincere. These old horse biddies were nice to their horses, even nicer to their dogs, but not so nice to each other. I was getting to the point where if I saw a lady over the age of forty-five in riding clothes, I wanted to run for my life.

"Oh, we're so happy, too. Thank you. She'll be taking the horse Idle Dice."

"I see. I'm actually here to talk to the girl who rode Idle Dice a few weeks ago. Is she here today?"

Martha paused.

I held my breath. What else was I going to get in trouble for?

"She should be."

Martha didn't know what had happened.

I came out from behind my car.

"This is Sid," said Martha.

"Hi, Sidney. I'm Madeline Cardwell from USEF."

"Hi," I said. I was going to be fined or sanctioned or never allowed to show again. This day was spelling nothing but doom.

"There's room for one more entry in the Maclay Finals. One rider had to scratch, so we'll take one more from the regionals, and you're next on the list."

I just stared at her.

"Sidney?" she said.

"What?" I asked. My brain was numb.

"You qualified for the Maclay Finals."

"My! Congratulations!" said Martha. Madeline Cardwell handed me an envelope.

"Here's your official letter. Please call me if you have any questions."

They were both smiling at me. I opened the letter. There was a USEF seal at the top, and sure enough, I was being invited to ride in the finals.

Kelly came out of the barn.

"She just qualified for the Garden," Martha told her.

Kelly's mouth fell open. Then she asked, "What are you going to ride?"

"I don't . . . I don't know," I stammered.

She looked at me for a long time, and I finally took a breath.

"You know, you're only as good as your horse," Kelly said.

"No, Kelly, your horse is only as good as you," I said.

And I got in my car and left.

TWENTY-SIX

IT STARTED TO pour as I was driving over Afton Mountain. I got behind a tractor-trailer heaving slowly uphill with its hazards on. The right lane was blocked off because of falling rocks — pieces of a smashed boulder lay behind orange construction webbing. I took my foot off the gas, feeling the frustration build. Couldn't I just get up the damn mountain?

If I'd known I'd qualified, I wouldn't have mouthed off. I might even have sucked up a little to Martha to borrow a horse from them — that was how badly I wanted to go to New York.

I stopped by my house and got some things for Wayne. I wanted to make him dinner, figured we could talk over some warm food.

When I got to his house, he was sitting at his table halfway into a fifth of bourbon, smoking a cigarette and staring at the television. He looked horrible. This bender was getting worse.

"I'm making you a redneck casserole — tuna fish and corn flakes," I said, opening a cabinet.

He didn't say anything.

"I got fired from the barn."

He looked up. "What for?"

"Mouthing off."

"Ain't that a surprise." He shook his head, getting upset. "Damn it, girl, don't you know when to keep it shut? Talk about cutting off your nose to spite your face. That was your chance to make something of yourself."

"Look who's talking," I said.

I pulled the letter out of my pocket and handed it to him.

"What is it?"

I didn't answer. He found his glasses and opened it.

He read it, then looked up at me.

"I guess I'm lucky they let me qualify."

"It ain't a goddamn lottery. It ain't luck. You earned it."

"I'm not going to find a horse!" I slammed the cabinet and yelled so loudly that he jumped. "I could be great if I had people helping me and if I had a great horse, but I don't."

That was like a knife in his heart, I could tell. It wasn't like he didn't know it already, but I was sure he didn't want to hear it out loud.

He took a long look at me. "I can get you a horse."

I ignored him.

"You hear what I said?"

"You would, wouldn't you? You'd sell me some old nag, and you'd let me take him to New York City. Because you're a drunken fool."

Wayne looked at me hard and pointed his finger. "Oh, so now you all fancy? Well, let me tell you something you don't know: I went to the National Hunter Finals in Atlanta, Georgia, and showed a horse myself. She was off the track six months. I was fifteen and lied about my age. I jumped that crazy bitch over four-and-a-half-foot jumps in front of five thousand people, and I came in tenth out of forty-one. Not too bad. So when that fancy coach talks about how much he knows, let me ask you how many horses he's ridden in the middle of downtown Atlanta, half-drunk, at fifteen."

"You're lying," I said.

"The hell I am. Rode down in a boxcar with my lunch in a paper sack. You ask your mama if it's true."

I knew when he was lying, and I knew when he wasn't. This was a true story. I started mixing up the casserole. Wayne opened a drawer, dug through some papers, pulled out a framed photograph, and handed it to me. It was Wayne as a grinning, big-eared teenager on a gorgeous dapple gray horse, holding a big ribbon. It gave me the shivers. It was just an old photo, but for some reason it made me want to cry.

"Sidney, you're a catch rider. We'll find you a horse."

"I ain't got a coach."

"I'll do it."

"You're a drunk."

"I'll quit."

"Sure you will."

I set the timer for thirty minutes and put the dish in the oven. I got my coat. I knew if I stuck around, we'd fight.

"You be here tomorrow, rain or shine."

I walked out and the door slammed behind me.

I didn't want to go home, but I had to. All afternoon, along with everything else, I'd been thinking about Melinda and worrying that Donald was going to hurt her. I couldn't turn my back on her, as mean as she had been to me the night before and as much as it broke my heart. I was just too loyal, kind of like a dumb old dog. Between her and Dee Dee, it seemed mothers were put on this earth just to torture their kids. To find the softest spot in your heart and jam their thumb into it. I knew that all mothers weren't like this. I knew my mother hadn't always been like this. Jimmy never would have married her if she had been. I felt like Donald and I were fighting for her soul.

TWENTY-SEVEN

I SPENT THE NIGHT at home, went to school the next day, and dragged through my classes. I decided to go to Wayne's, like he'd said, and see what he could come up with. The drunk he was on had to be over by now.

But when I got to his house and opened the door, I found him lying face-down on the floor. I put my hand on him — he was unconscious but breathing. His feet were pointed in, pigeon-toed, and he looked like a doll someone had thrown across the room. Boy, it was horrible seeing him like that. I called 911, and then I just waited, holding his hand and listening to the pot of water sizzling and popping on the wood stove. The fire was about two hours old, but I didn't know how long he'd been lying there.

An ambulance pulled into the muddy driveway. It looked so wrong there, its lights flashing as it drove past the tractors and wheelbarrows. Two men got out — one I knew from church and one worked at the farmer's co-op. They came in and checked him out, put an oxygen mask on him. They said his heart rate was slow. The older one said he was dehydrated and started an IV.

"This Wayne Stewart, the horse trader?" the boy asked. The other fellow nodded but let me answer.

"Yeah," I said.

"He went to school with my daddy. Tough as a mule. They used to bootleg together, but don't tell no one." He smiled.

"He going to be okay?" My voice caught.

"He looks right frail. We'll see."

I drove to the hospital behind them. Inside, I followed the gurney down the hall and sat in the waiting area.

A few minutes later, Melinda came flying in the door. "Why didn't you call me? What the hell is wrong with you?"

"I didn't want you to bring that dirtbag," I said.

"Well, it's a good thing Sandy heard it over the scanner."

"Good for her."

"Is he okay?"

"Don't know."

She sat down and stared at me.

A doctor came out and told us we could follow him into Wayne's room. Wayne looked awful, but he was awake.

"Your liver ain't getting any better," the doctor said.

"I just quit drinking," Wayne rasped.

"When?"

"Yesterday."

"Should have done it thirty years ago."

"So now I just lie here and die?"

"Don't be getting mad at me, Wayne. I been telling you for a long time. You might drop dead in a month, you might live ten years."

The doctor left, and we all just sat there awhile without saying anything.

"You know, I been making casseroles for you for forty years," Melinda said finally.

"Maybe that's what did it," Wayne said without missing a beat.

She stood up. "I been waking up every day wondering if you fell asleep with a cigarette and burned the house down!" she shouted. "Or if you finally drunk yourself to death. You're so lucky to be alive, and you just want to die."

He reached over slowly and took a sip of water from a plastic cup. "We was born to a mom and dad who didn't want us," he said. "The fact that we survived is lucky enough."

"We didn't survive," she said. I felt kind of bad hearing that. Then Melinda turned to me and said, "You need to stop wasting your time shoveling shit and get a real job."

"Look who's talking," I said.

"Horses are the biggest money pit God ever created. How many times did your father say we were broke, then spend his paycheck on a load of hay? Sidney, you need to get to school and make something of yourself."

"So I can take care of you?" I asked her. "Is that why?"

"I'm going home." She put her coat on and grabbed her purse. "You know, I had dreams, too, Sidney. In case you forgot, the night Daddy died, I was going to sign a lease to open a sewing store, remember?"

"No."

"Of course you don't."

She left. I did remember the sewing store.

Wayne and I were silent for a long time. I counted the drops of fluid in his IV so I wouldn't cry.

Wayne opened his eyes and looked at me, then closed them again. "We're going to the Garden," he said.

"Shut up."

"We're doing this for you."

"I could give a shit about the Garden."

"I'm going there, and you're going with me. You got a chance to win the National Championship, girl."

I didn't say anything. I hoped I wouldn't die like that, lying in a hospital bed with everybody fighting and telling me how dumb I was for doing the things I did. All the people Wayne knew, all the horses he had, all that knowledge he had, and one day he'd just die and all of it would be gone. It couldn't happen to me. I didn't think I'd mind being dead — it was the dying part that scared me.

Wayne had opened his eyes and was staring at me. "Sidney, I don't know how much longer I'm gonna be around. I ain't in good shape."

"You better not drop dead and leave me here alone with these people. I'll kill you myself."

And then, goddamn it, I started to cry.

"You can't leave me, Uncle Wayne."

"Let's go to New York," he said. "We got three weeks."

TWENTY-EIGHT

THE NEXT DAY, Ruthie came out to Wayne's to help me feed. She'd been there a couple of times to watch me ride. We were walking through the deep mud carrying hay. She was grossed out because her feet were making sucking sounds in the mud.

"How's he live like this?" she asked me.

"He could live in a hollow log. Give those horses a bale, too, but break it up so they don't fight over it."

"Okay. You heard about Eileen Cleek?" she asked.

"What about her?"

"She dropped out of school to work in the mill."

I stopped in my tracks. It had to be a joke.

"Is that sad or what?" Ruthie said. "She was the last real farm girl, except you. I heard some girls saying she would either be pregnant or cooking meth by the end of the school year."

"That's not funny."

"I know it isn't."

Ruthie threw a clump of hay into the paddock. The horses fought each other for it, ears pinned and teeth bared.

"I said to split it up. They'll kick the crap out of each other!"

I let the horses rip off clumps of hay and drag it off to eat.

"They're scary!" Ruthie looked down at her filthy clothes. "Can we go in now?"

"We gotta pick out all of these horses' feet or they'll get thrush. They been standing out here in the mud for two days."

"What's 'flush'?"

"Thrush. It's a nasty fungus. Smells awful."

"Yuck!" Ruthie looked at Sub, who was covered in manure stains.

"And we have to soak that red horse's foot."

I called to Sub.

"Why's he called Sub?"

"Short for Submarine 'cause he likes to swim in the river. One time my daddy . . ."

I choked up. Everything was falling apart.

"Your daddy what?"

"One time my daddy and I were riding him together, crossing the Jackson River, and Sub put his head down and went underwater like a fish. So we changed his name to Submarine. He got us soaking wet."

I could tell Ruthie wanted me to keep talking.

"If my father came back tomorrow, he'd drag Donald out

by his hair. And he wouldn't be too happy with my mother, either."

I looked at Sub for a moment, and he looked back. He walked over to me, rested his head on my shoulder, and closed his eyes. His cheekbone sank into the top of my shoulder, and I thought he was going to push me over with that big head of his.

"Aww — look at him. He's so quiet," Ruthie said.

"He is. And it's catching."

I scraped some of the dried mud off his cheek. Then I turned my back and walked away.

Ruthie and I cleaned up the barn without talking for a while. I could tell she was thinking about something.

"You know, Sid, I wasn't sure if I should tell you, but I heard Daddy saying some things about Donald."

"Like what? Like that he's evil incarnate?"

"Like he used to hit his girlfriend over in Elkins. Daddy's worried that he might hit your mom."

I turned and faced Ruthie. "Ruthie, he hit *me*."

Once the words came out of my mouth, everything changed. It was real. It was out.

"You have to tell your mother and Wayne. If you don't, I'll tell my father, he'll call Wayne, and the shit will hit the holy fan," she said.

I almost wished I hadn't said anything, but it felt good knowing she cared so much that she actually threatened me.

I didn't know who else I was going to tell or what I was going to do, but I had to do something. I knew Ruthie would do what she'd said. That was how Ruthie was. She left without saying anything.

Melinda and I picked up Wayne from the hospital, and she drove us to his house in her car. I thought about telling her then, but I couldn't. I was scared she would pick Donald over me — that was why I had kept it secret in the first place. I was scared she wouldn't believe me or that she would believe me but not really care. Sometimes I didn't know what went on in her head, but I knew I loved her no matter what.

Melinda helped Wayne inside and made him some tea, and then she went home. Wayne's neighbor Marlene Watson came by with a hot dish of food and talked for a while. She lived down the road and ran a cattle farm with her husband, who used to work at the mill as a pipe fitter but had retired. She had a cheerful face, like a daisy, and it made me feel good just looking at her. After she left, another neighbor, Pete Carter, a used-car dealer in Hot Springs, came by to say hello. He was a round and neatly dressed man with his pants pulled all the way up around the top of his giant belly, and he looked at you out of little slit eyes behind his metal-rimmed glasses.

Pete and Wayne told stories about when they were young. The first one was about the time they were out of work when they were eighteen. They tied a long rag to a fox's tail, dipped it in kerosene, and let the fox run through the woods. They said it was rigged so the rag would fall off and the fox wouldn't get hurt. They started a big forest fire, so they would get hired to put it out. When they were twelve, they tied a lit stick of dynamite to a buzzard to see what would happen. It crawled under Wayne's uncle's brand-new Cadillac and they thought the whole thing was going to blow, until they found the fuse lying there limply by their feet. Pete told one about how he and his brother-in-law got drunk and used a coffee can to spray-paint big red polka dots all over their boss's new truck.

They laughed until they coughed. Then it got real quiet, and we listened to the fire.

"Yeah. I ain't had a drink in ten years," said Pete.

"Is that so?" asked Wayne.

"Ain't got no use for it," Pete said. After a few moments, he got up. "You need anything, you call me." He put his hand on Wayne's shoulder, as if he knew it was serious.

I'd been waiting to talk to Wayne about Donald. But I didn't know how to bring it up. I felt bad that he was sick and that I was going to upset him. I didn't know what to do.

I sat in the armchair by the wood stove. Wayne put another log on the fire and lay back down on the couch.

"Ruthie's daddy said Donald used to hit his girlfriend when he lived over in Elkins," I said.

Wayne's neck snapped around so fast that I almost jumped out of my chair.

"Earl said that?"

I nodded, scared. Was it really such a surprise? I couldn't make myself tell him the rest.

Wayne took a deep, long breath. "I tried to tell her he was good-for-nothing. But she don't listen," he said.

Right about then I wanted him to say that he would go over and take care of that son of a bitch.

"You know, Sidney, it might be time just to let your mama go."

I sat there, biting my lip, trying not to say anything or cry, and he fell asleep.

TWENTY-NINE

About three hours later, I woke up and Wayne wasn't there. I jumped up and looked out the window, and he was standing by the riding ring. He'd rigged up lights to illuminate the ring in the dark. It was a heck of a splice job, with wires sticking out and lights teetering on ladders.

I ran outside. "You're supposed to be in bed!" I said.

"Now we're a twenty-four-hour facility," he said proudly.

"You're going to electrocute all of us."

"We can train in the dark, after work. Get the horse used to lights."

"What horse?"

"You'll see."

I looked at him.

"I made a couple calls," he said.

I wondered what he was up to. Beezie didn't have any eq horses, and she wouldn't let him borrow something half-baked to take to the finals, just on principle. But he had a network of moonshine buddies, horse traders, mule skinners, farriers, tree pruners, blacksmiths, bricklayers, roofers, cattle farmers, deer hunters, bear hunters, fiddlers, banjo pickers, trout fishermen, you name it. And then there were the good old boys who did just about everything. It didn't matter if he'd talked to them in the past twenty years or not. He could call old So-and-So and talk for half an hour, then ask, "Do you got old So-and-So's number?" and he'd be on the phone with whoever he wanted in a day or two.

We went back to the house as it was getting dark.

"You wearing your heart monitor?" I asked.

He pulled up his shirt and showed me the wires. "I'm the electric horseman."

We fell asleep by the wood stove.

THIRTY

Headlights flashed by, and I woke up and looked out the window. The car passed. The clock said 2:45. I closed my eyes again.

I didn't know how much time went by. Then bright lights flooded the room again.

Wayne woke up.

A pickup truck pulling a cattle trailer came crunching down the driveway, its headlights bouncing off the mist and sending the cat tearing under the porch.

Wayne got up and looked out the window. "There he is."

"You're having my fancy horse delivered in a cattle trailer? Boy, you sure know how to impress."

But Wayne was already out the door.

A big man got out of the truck — clean coveralls, round face, beard. Hunting season was coming, and the hunters had stopped shaving.

"Howdy there," he said.

"Sidney, this is Chew-Gum." Sure enough, he was

chewing gum. "Chew-Gum's from over in Lewisburg." West Virginia. The Other Side.

Chew-Gum looked at the lights Wayne had rigged up. "Boy, that's some contraption you got thar."

"You can see, canchyee?" said Wayne. Chew-Gum's thick accent was catching.

"I reckon."

Wayne looked at his watch. "You sure ain't in no hurry, Chew-Gum."

"Sorry 'bout that. Had to replace the carburetor on the truck. Had the horse all loaded up and ever-thang."

"What you waiting for? I want to see the horse."

Chew-Gum unlocked the trailer and swung the door open. He climbed in, went around behind the horse, and pushed the horse off the ledge, like he was unloading a steer. No fancy ramps here. The horse jumped down. He was a big, light bay with two white socks, shaggy around the feet and ears, and sweaty. He had a friendly face with a white strip. Equitation horses were usually solid colored without any white even on their feet, so as not to distract the judges. He was not broke, no way, and I knew he was no equitation horse.

I knew it would be like that. I knew it. But I hadn't known it would be quite this bad.

"This here is Mystical Tour. After that old Beatles song, "Magical Mystery —"

"I know," I said.

"This here is the great-great-grandson of Secretariat. But they lost his papers."

"Bullshit," I muttered.

"He's one hundred percent sound, levelheaded."

"You're telling me this is an equitation horse?"

"Well, here's the thing, Sidney. This horse will jump any dang thing you put in front of him. We done tried it. He jumped over a tractor. He just loves to jump. And he ain't got a wee-kid bone in his body."

Chew-Gum said "wee-kid" instead of "wicked," so he must have been from down near Clinch Mountain. A tractor? He was lying and I knew it. Wayne kept a stone-cold poker face and chewed on a toothpick. I could see he wasn't buying this one bit, either.

"I seen him jump out of the field," Chew-Gum said. "He sprang my pony and they ran all the way down to Route Twelve damn near Piercys Mill before I caught them. But here's the main thing. He's a smooth ride, got the easiest jump you ever saw — a little flat, maybe, so he wouldn't make a jumper. He's got a rocking-horse canter, and he's got a background as a show hunter but no papers. Wayne tells me you're looking for a equitation horse, a horse that you can count on and that makes you look good. Well, here you go."

Good equitation horses went for around a hundred and fifty thousand dollars. And here I was looking at something off a cattle trailer without any papers. Maybe we'd fix him up and sell him. I ran my hands down his cannon bones, feeling for splints or anything else.

"Oh, he's sound," Chew-Gum said as I looked at the bottom of the horse's hooves and in his mouth. He had a bad wolf tooth — a useless tooth that about half of all horses get right next to their premolars — but we could pull it. He seemed clean otherwise.

"Trot him out for me, Sidney," Wayne said.

I jogged alongside the horse away from them. Wayne studied the horse's trot. Then Chew-Gum trotted him so I could see.

"Well, he ain't lame," Wayne said.

"Of course he ain't," said Chew-Gum.

Somebody had to ask. Better if it was me. "You didn't give him anything, did you?"

"Hell no," he said, offended.

"He paddles with his front left," I said to Wayne. Paddling is what it's called when horses overcompensate for being pigeon-toed.

"A little."

"A little? He paddles like a duck," I said.

"Probably his shoes," Wayne said. He picked up one of the horse's hooves and inspected it. "Hey, you got this horse shod to plow a field or what?" he said to Chew-Gum.

"Yeah, I threw on some big steel shoes I had. Not the best, I reckon."

Wayne thought, chewed on his toothpick. "His heels aren't trimmed evenly on his front left. I reckon that's why he's paddling."

"Yeah, I reckon." Chew-Gum eyed Sub, who was standing in the paddock half-asleep. "I'll give you a thousand for that pinto."

"He ain't for sale," said Wayne.

"So, what do you think of this fella?" asked Chew-Gum, nodding toward the new horse.

"We'll try him out for a week."

"All right. But don't turn him out in the field with anyone — they'll be mincemeat by morning." We said goodbye, and Chew-Gum got into his trailer and left.

"He was lying his ass off," I said.

"Don't worry. I known him all my life."

"That's what I'm afraid of," I said.

Wayne shook his head. "A thousand dollars for Submarine. That boy's so cheap, he wouldn't pay a nickel to see Jesus Christ ride a bicycle."

I put the new horse in a stall and gave him a flake of hay.

"He paddles like a duck," I said. "He's got a wolf tooth. No one's seen him jump. His head is so high, he'll give you a bloody nose if you're not careful. This ain't the horse."

"Not if you talk about him like that," Wayne said.

"You're the one who always said, 'You can put your boots in the oven. That don't make 'em biscuits.'"

Wayne put on his heavy blacksmith's chaps and grabbed a set of farrier's pliers. He picked up the horse's front left hoof, pulled the shoe off, started to trim and file. "We'll see how he goes with some better shoes."

I looked at the shoes he was going to use. "Where'd you get those?"

"They were throwing them out at the barn."

"They're aluminum."

He handed one to me. "Feel how light they are."

I felt the shoe. Light as a feather. "Throwing them out, huh?"

"And they got ridges on them so he don't slip. Probably cost a hundred bucks each. Hey, how's that tooth?"

"We need to get it out before we can put a bridle on him," I said. "That must hurt, rubbing up against the bit."

Wayne looked at the tooth and got me some pliers out of his tool bag. "Yank that thing on outta there. Real quick." He grabbed the horse's top lip as hard as he could to distract him and braced himself against the wall with the other hand. The horse snorted and his eyes popped open wide.

"Got him?" I asked.

"Yep. Get in there."

I reached into the horse's mouth, clamped the pliers down on the tooth, and ripped it out. The horse sat back on his haunches and slammed into the wall behind him.

Wayne looked down at the pliers in my hand with the horse's brown tooth.

"Good girl."

The horse shook his head hard when Wayne let him go.

"You can rinse now, mister," I said.

We decided to let him spend the night in a paddock by himself, resting and getting used to things. He'd be mad after having his tooth pulled. I'd get on him the next day.

He had good enough manners not to pull away from the halter as I unbuckled it. I turned him out in the paddock and he trotted away. We watched him sniff the ground and check out the other horses. "Wayne, you can't teach a horse to jump a three-and-a-half-foot fence in a few weeks and then compete in a national championship."

"Sure you can."

"This might be a good horse someday, but he ain't our horse."

"We'll see," he said.

I decided to sleep the rest of the night at home. Driving away from the farm in the dark, I looked at the horse one last time in the rearview mirror. He was trotting back and forth, trying to get out. I glanced at the road in front of me, and then I glanced back, and damned if that horse didn't jump a four-foot fence out of that paddock!

I slammed on the brakes and got out to see Wayne frozen in midstep, watching the horse trot to the barn.

"You see that?" he said.

"Yeah!" I said. "He snapped those knees up so tight, you couldn't even see his feet."

I walked right over and caught him standing by the barn. We tacked him up, and I climbed on while Wayne set up a couple of fences. The horse tossed the bit around, waiting for it to hit his wolf tooth, and then he let it rest against the bars of his mouth and ignored it. I trotted him around, cantered him in a circle. You could tell that he was a little fresh and hadn't been worked in a while, but I just couldn't believe how smooth he was. I aimed him at a jump in the center of the ring and he cleared it with a foot to spare.

"Well, goddamn, Chew-Gum!" Wayne said, and laughed a loud "Ha!" that I hadn't heard in a long time.

We kept jumping. His jump was a little flat, meaning he didn't toss me out of the saddle too hard, so my form looked better.

"He don't even raise an eyebrow," Wayne said.

"He ain't paddling with those new shoes, and he snaps his knees up real tight," I said.

We kept jumping and, I swear, that horse just got better and better.

Finally we quit and let the horse out for the night.

We went inside, and I lay down on the couch and turned out the light. Wayne fell asleep by the stove. I looked out the window and watched the horse in the moonlight, shuffling around the paddock, and I hoped he'd still be there in the morning.

THIRTY-ONE

SINCE CHEW-GUM HADN'T told us the new horse's barn name, we decided to call him Sonny after Sonny Osborne, Wayne's favorite bluegrass singer. The next day, I fired up the big Oster clippers, oiled the blades, and clipped Sonny from head to tail. That way, if we did wind up going to the finals, his hair would have time to grow in. If we cut it too close to the show date, he'd have clippers marks and would look ridiculous. As the strips of brown hair slid off, his cuts and scrapes looked a lot worse. I brushed off all the loose hair and rubbed mineral oil into the scars. Wayne and I decided to feed him a mix of protein sweet feed with some mineral oil for his coat and some pellets. No corn, though, or else he'd get so fired up that he'd jump over the damn barn.

Wayne went back to Oak Hill. I felt bad being left behind, and I missed talking to Wes. I missed Edgar and the other stable hands. Wayne told me Kelly was schooling every day for the finals, and she was taking three horses: Idle Dice, her gelding, and a new hundred-and-fifty-thousand-dollar Oldenburg equitation horse.

When I heard that, I went to Wayne's and groomed the heck out of Sonny. I pulled his mane, untangled his tail, and scrubbed him to within an inch of his life. I clipped his whiskers with the little clippers, trimmed his ears and around his jaw. I rubbed mineral oil into his eyelids and nose. I rubbed Hooflex into his hooves and wrapped his legs. And then, when I was done with Sonny, I started working on the other horses. I was determined not to let Wayne's horses look scruffy and neglected anymore. I even clipped Submarine and started giving him mineral oil — don't ask me why.

I found an old New Zealand horse blanket in Wayne's attic. It had mouse holes, but I taped them up with duct tape and started turning Sonny out in it to protect his coat.

One day we set up a tough course for Sonny. Before I mounted up, Wayne called me over to where he stood in the center of our makeshift ring.

"You know the difference between soft eyes and hard eyes?" Wayne asked me. I shook my head.

"Look straight ahead at that jump." He walked in a semicircle away from me, toward the edge of my vision. "Tell me when I'm out of your sight."

"Now," I said.

"That's it? You can't see me?"

"No."

"You're looking with hard eyes. Now, relax your eyes and let them take in everything in front of you. You're still looking at the jump, but with soft eyes. See all the things in the corners of your vision — on the edges."

"Okay."

"*Now,* tell me when you can't see me." He walked around next to me again, but I could still see him, so I waited a bit.

"Okay, now."

"Well, that's a lot better."

"Yeah."

"When you're in the ring, riding the course, use your soft eyes. See everything. See the jump in front of you, but rest your eyes. When you rest your eyes, the horse can relax. He knows you got it."

I wondered why he'd never told me this before.

"Remember, they're judging you, not him. But if he makes a mistake, they're going to decide whether it was his mistake or yours. If he trips, was it just a stumble, or were you letting him get away from you? Were you underriding? Were you overriding?"

"You ain't as dumb as I thought," I said.

He laughed. "Let me tell you *something.*"

This was how he started a lecture. Sometimes it was "Let me tell you *something you don't know.*"

"A horseman is somebody who can break a horse, jump a horse, shoe a horse, breed a horse, work with any kind of horse, any problem, any age. When I was a kid, I rode on trail rides for fun, we jumped in the ring, I went along on fox hunts at Folly Farm, I rode in shows, I rode in a steeplechase. I done everything. Nowadays, these show barns get the top blacksmith, the top vet. You got a trainer for the jumpers and another trainer for the hunters. It's specialized because they all want to be perfect. They all want to be the perfect equitation rider or the perfect pony rider or create the perfect working hunter or the perfect pleasure horse. But the best rider is the rider who can ride anything. The best rider is a catch rider."

I hadn't heard him put it all together like that before.

"I want to be a catch rider," I said.

"Then you gotta get on anything, any horse, and you gotta find a way to make it work."

When we were done with the course, I turned Sonny out into the field. He trotted nervously along the rail of the fence, back and forth.

"He's lonely. Get that donkey," Wayne said.

I put a halter on Mr. Wilcox, brought him in, and turned him loose with Sonny, who sniffed the donkey and tried to bite him. The donkey pinned his ears, spun around, backed up to kick Sonny, and squealed bloody murder.

"Get that thing outta there before he rips the horse to pieces!" Wayne hollered, but he was already doing it himself. "That is the bitingest donkey I ever seen!" He grabbed the donkey by the nose with one hand and behind the ears with the other and took him down, right to the ground. When the donkey got up, Wayne shoved him into the other paddock. That donkey was as ornery as they come, but I could tell Wayne was stuck with him because, although he would never admit it, he liked him. Unless that donkey tried to stomp him in the head — which some of them will do — Wayne would keep him.

"What about Sub?" I asked.

Wayne nodded.

I put Sub in with Sonny and watched them sniff each other. Sub nosed the pile of hay, and Sonny watched him with his ears up. They sniffed each other some more, and Sonny squealed and kicked out with his hind leg as if to say, "See, I can kick," but Sub just ignored it, so we knew they'd get along.

THIRTY-TWO

"We're leaving in four days. I think you should get out of the ring and take him for a ride. Then we let him rest."

Time had flown by. I hadn't been to school for more than a week. We had made the hotel reservation, done the entry forms, and planned the trip up to New York. Wayne had spent more money than I wanted to think about. I promised myself I would pay him back someday.

Wayne had changed the oil in the truck and replaced the brake pads, gotten two good used tires, and rewired the trailer so the brake lights came on when they were supposed to. He installed some Plexiglas inside the trailer so the wind wouldn't bother the horse too much if it got cold on the highway.

We were talking about all the things we still had to do when I saw a blue truck pull in and realized that it was Wes.

"Boy, you lost?" said Wayne, smiling.

"What are you doing all the way over here?" I said.

"I had to look at a horse in Goshen. Some half quarter horse, half Belgian they were using to pull a buckboard."

"How's his feet?" asked Wayne.

"Exactly," said Wes.

Quarter horses can have soft little feet, and with the extra weight of a Belgian draft horse — Belgians have their own hoof issues — that could lead to trouble.

Wes got out of his truck. "I heard you guys are headed to New York. Pretty brave of you, Sid."

I didn't know what to say. I tied Sonny's lead shank up to an eyehook. He moved his haunches around to the side so he could look at Wes.

"I'm sorry about what happened," he said.

"It ain't your fault," I said.

"I know it ain't. But, you know, her mother is just wicked sometimes."

"Her mother didn't fire me."

"I know. But that's where it all comes from."

I turned away from him to pick Sonny's feet. "You drove all the way over here to tell me what a nice person she is?"

"I know she don't have the right to act like that," he admitted. He put his hands in his pockets and changed the subject. "This your horse?"

I nodded.

"I like the look of him."

"Thanks. He's honest, and that's all I can ask for."

"That is pretty much everything, ain't it?" he asked. "How's his jump?"

"Terrific."

I showed Wes around Wayne's place, introduced all the horses, and showed him the cattle in the lower field.

I saw the red horse picking a fight with one of the ponies. I noticed that when he trotted away, he didn't look lame anymore. Wes and I went out into the field and caught him. Wes was so gentle with the horse that the horse picked up his foot to show Wes before Wes had even touched him.

I got Wes to trot the horse out for me. The gelding was sound, but he'd lost some muscle tone. Wes suggested I move him to the paddock on the hill so he'd build up his shoulders and hindquarters as he grazed up and down the slope. He said that since he was a quiet, straightforward horse and had such a big jump, he might make a nice field hunter. I figured I could trailer him to Beezie's and work him on her cross-country course after the finals.

Wes looked at his watch and said he had to leave.

"Well, good luck, Sid. You earned it. I'll see you there."

Driving home that night in the dark, I didn't know what to think about Wes, but I sure was glad he'd come over. No boy had ever talked to me like he did. He listened to what I said, like he thought it was important. I wasn't used to that. Sometimes when I looked him in the eye, he looked away, like he was shy. I wasn't used to that, either.

I walked into the house and decided not to lock horns with Donald because I didn't want to get distracted. I wasn't going to let him take all of this away from me. I still didn't know who to tell about him hitting me. I would keep my promise to Ruthie, but I didn't know how.

Donald was eating at the table. My mother came out of the kitchen. "We have dinner if you want it," she said.

"I'll pass," I said, looking at him. I should have been more polite, but when I saw him, I just couldn't.

Sure enough, he grabbed me by the arm and just about threw me into a chair. Melinda rushed at him, and he pushed her away so hard that she slammed into the corner cupboard.

Without thinking about it — although I'd thought about it a hundred times — I ran into my room and got the .44 out from under my bedsprings. It was waiting there for me. I felt like I was in a movie as I picked it up and wrapped my hand around the grip.

I walked out into the living room, where Melinda was backing away from him. He reached up to grab her by the face, and I pointed the pistol at his head. He turned to look at me, and so did she.

I clicked the safety off. *Snap.*

Donald froze. His mouth was slightly open.

"Girl . . ." he said.

There was a long pause. I watched his hands and feet to make sure he didn't make a move. I was good at this. Then the words just came out of me, very calm. "My daddy went to the store one day and never came home. I didn't think my life could get any worse. But you sure found a way."

"If you were my daughter, I'd — "

"Sidney, give it to me," Melinda said.

"No."

"Sidney."

"He hit me, Mama. He hit me in the face."

"Now."

"That's a lie," he said.

"It ain't a lie. It's the truth. He knocked me down on the floor. I didn't tell you because I was scared you wouldn't believe me." My voice broke. "Or that you would believe me and you wouldn't care."

Donald started to reach for me, but I looked down the barrel of that pistol right at his head and he stopped cold.

Melinda watched me, breathing through her mouth, not moving a muscle.

"You let her run this house," Donald said to Melinda. "You're the one who ought to smack her once in a while."

Suddenly, Melinda faced him. In almost a whisper, she said, "You get out of my house now, and if I ever see you near my daughter, I'll kill you myself."

My heart nearly jumped out of my chest.

Donald looked at his hot dinner, sat down, and reached

to take a bite, and I almost couldn't believe what happened next. She took his dinner plate and threw it at him.

He jumped up, bellowing. "You'll never find a man, Melinda Criser. You're going to wind up a dried-up old bitch all by yourself."

"I'll take my chances," she said.

He looked toward the cabinet in the living room. "I'm going to Bakersfield," he said. "You want to live here in this shit hole — "

"You thinking about your knives, ain't you?" She laughed. "I'll mail them to you in Bakersfield." I didn't know if she was serious. "But you set foot near this house or near either one of us again, like I said, I'll kill you."

"You're both crazy as shit."

"*Get out!*" she roared, and I nearly jumped a foot.

He walked out to his truck, started it up, and tore away, spinning gravel. When the sound of the truck had died out, Melinda reached for the gun. I pulled it away from her. "If you think I'm sleeping without this tonight, you really are crazy," I said.

"I got my own," she said. "But we gotta get rid of those knives tonight."

I wanted to ask her what the hell she had her own gun for if she wasn't going to use it on a shit heel like Donald, but instead I went to the cabinet and pulled out the knives.

I wrapped them in a bath towel and gave them to her. We walked together down the hill toward Route 220 and she shoved them down a storm drain. I heard the clatter below.

"I hope some sewer rat don't find them. He'll come get us," I joked.

"Ain't no one going to use those knives," she said. "They'll be down there a long time, rusting."

When we got home, Melinda locked the doors and windows and closed the curtains. She got all of Donald's stuff together — his clothes, his magazines, everything — and made a pile at the end of the driveway. I helped her clean up the food on the floor. She poured herself a glass of whiskey, drank it, and went to bed.

I didn't know what she was thinking, but it had to be a lot of things. I figured she was scared and relieved and kind of sick about everything.

I was jumpy that night. Every time a car drove by, I looked out the window. I kept thinking I saw Donald lurking behind a tree.

The next morning my eyes burned from no sleep. I went into the kitchen and made eggs, put two frozen waffles in the toaster. Melinda got up when she heard me in there, and she looked as though she hadn't slept, either.

"I'm changing all the locks," she said. "But I want us to sleep at Wayne's for a few days."

Melinda drove us to Wayne's in my car. I couldn't

remember the last time she'd driven me anywhere, and it felt good not to be the one driving. We wound up toward Hot Springs, along the Jackson River, and I just stared out the window.

We told Wayne what had happened. When Melinda said that Donald had hit me, he stumbled backwards as though someone had shoved him, and said, "Hmmmmph!" He was silent for about ten seconds while we held our breath. Then he pounded his fist so hard on the kitchen table that I heard a piece of wood snap. "Why didn't you tell me?" Wayne shouted at me.

"That ain't the question," Melinda said. "The question is why didn't she tell *me,* and the answer is that she was trying to." Her face was trembling.

I have to admit, I liked that they were all worked up and upset, finally seeing what I had been seeing and finally carrying what I had been carrying. It was their job to deal with this, not mine. They had been too busy thinking about themselves. Now they were stunned like hornets who'd woken up on a cold morning, nearly frozen, crawling around with their stingers curled up underneath them, not knowing what to do.

I went into the other room to watch television, and they stayed in the kitchen to put dishes away. I could hear them talking.

"You're only going to have one day in New York before the show?" she asked. "Most people take three or four to get the horses used to it."

"Can't afford it, Melinda."

"I know," she said.

"She can do it," he said.

They cleaned up for a few more minutes.

She spoke again. "How long before I stop worrying he's gonna come get us while we're sleeping?"

"To tell you the truth," Wayne said, "I think he's too much of a chickenshit."

And then I heard her laugh—"Ha!"—just the way Wayne did. They sounded exactly alike.

THIRTY-THREE

THAT NIGHT, I tried on my coat and breeches and polished the boots. Melinda knocked and opened the door. She looked at me like she wasn't sure I wanted her in there, and that made me feel bad.

"The coat's a little big in the waist," she said. "See — hold your arms out."

I held my arms out like a scarecrow and looked in the mirror. There was too much material hanging on the sides.

"Want me to take it in?"

"No time."

"I can do it."

There was a long silence after that. I couldn't remember the last time she'd done anything to help me, and my brain just froze.

"All right," I said at last. "If you're a hundred percent sure, because I don't have a backup."

"I'm a hundred percent sure," she said. "I tell you one

thing, your daddy would be riding up to New York with you and Wayne. He'd be so proud of you."

I wanted to be happy that she said that, but it made me kind of angry. "I wish you'd said this a long time ago. You've been letting that scumbag run our lives for a long time."

"Well, he's out, ain't he?"

"He's out 'cause I got him out," I said.

"If I'd known . . . I would have done it myself."

I wasn't sure she would have, but I knew she believed it.

"I'm sorry that's what it took."

I shrugged, not wanting to say any more and make her feel bad.

"Your daddy would want you to win."

She pinned the jacket and pulled the seams apart. She didn't have her sewing machine at Wayne's, but she told me she'd finish the coat before I left.

The next day, I met Ruthie for lunch and told her what had happened. She went with me to our house so I could get the sewing machine. Donald's stuff was still at the end of the driveway. I looked up and down the street for any sign of him.

Ruthie and I sat on the front porch and talked. She was mad at me for disappearing and not telling her what was going on. I said I was sorry. I told her my mother was exhausted and shaken up, and she said she would come by and check on her while I was gone. She wished me good luck and said to beat their pants off, and I laughed. Then I asked her what I'd been dreading: "Are you going away to boarding school?" She said she was. Some fancy school near Staunton. I felt my heart sink. She said she was coming home every weekend, and she made me promise her that we would do something together every Saturday. She asked if I would drive Dorine to school once I got my license, and I said I would, even though it would be a year or so.

She handed me a tiny box, and I opened it. It was a little piece of rose quartz on a thin gold chain. I put the necklace on and she fastened it for me.

"I found it on our trip to the Trueheart Mine. I thought it might bring you some good luck."

She looked shy when she said this, and I realized that it wasn't about luck at all. She was giving it to me so I wouldn't forget we were friends. But I knew we'd stay close, because things were always the same with us. She told me I could come visit her at boarding school and that there were a lot of horses at the school that I could ride.

On the way back to Wayne's, when I got to the top of the main road, I found myself peeling down toward the hollow, toward where June lived. I parked at the ram and walked through the woods. I knew where the house was — I could have found it blindfolded if a bear didn't get me first. I had absorbed the map of these woods by osmosis. I had learned that word in biology, and I loved it. Osmosis is when molecules move across a membrane on their own, without anyone pushing them. They just do it. I liked the idea of things happening on their own, without anyone pushing them.

The woods were very thick. June and his brother and sister wanted it that way so no one would find them, and they didn't clear the underbrush. I picked my way through the black locust, bull thistle hedges, and autumn olive. I knew that June had a trail somewhere but I couldn't see it. One time *National Geographic* came to look for the family, and the lady at the post office sent the reporters to the wrong hollow on purpose, just like the locals used to do to the revenuers back during Prohibition.

I saw smoke and knew I was almost there. I rounded a ridge and saw the little cabin. Boy, that wood fire smelled good. I wondered if they would invite me in and we'd sit down and eat biscuits together, like in a fairy tale.

Before I had taken another breath, there was a shotgun in my face. Maybelle was on the other end of it.

"Damn it, Maybelle, I'm Jimmy's daughter!"

"You ain't," she said in a high mountain squeak.

"The hell I ain't."

Maybelle was about eighty. She wore an old sweater and pants and men's boots. She had long gray hair and steely bright blue eyes that didn't even look real. Her face was so wrinkled that she looked like one of those apple-faced dolls that had been sitting in a closet too long.

June came out of the house, and then I saw the older brother, Clifford, behind the house chopping wood, his eyes on me like a hawk.

"June, tell your sister who I am," I said.

"That's Jimmy's girl, Maybelle!"

She lowered the shotgun. "I thought it was a b'ar," she said. "I was going to shoot him and can him for the winter." She smiled and showed her gums.

Good Lord, I thought. *Canning bear.* "I just wanted to —"

"Well, darn it, girl, I ain't seen you since you was about this tall." June held his hand out in front of him. He was lean, weathered and wrinkly, a little stooped, about seventy. He had a big toothless grin, thick glasses, and short gray hair that his brother must have trimmed for him.

I'd forgotten how chatty he was. Once he got to talking, he didn't stop. He was like a child living deep in the woods. He knew very little about life outside. One time, he spent the night on our couch because the next day was the beginning of revival week at the church. I got up in the middle of the night to find him watching static on the television, sitting up straight as a board, his eyes wide. He had never seen it before, and he couldn't look away. Boy, that gave me the shivers.

I remembered Wayne telling June about Jimmy's accident when June was standing outside the gas station eating a candy bar. He came out to buy one about three times a year. After Wayne told him, June took the candy bar and threw it away.

June seemed to read my mind now. He stopped talking and looked down at the dirt. "I bet you miss him something awful."

I nodded.

"I reckon it was his time."

"Sure didn't seem like it to me," I said.

June just looked up into the trees and we listened to a woodpecker.

"I'm going to New York City to show a horse in a couple days."

"What for?" he said, like I was telling him about some kind of tragedy.

"Wayne's taking me. We'll be back in a few days. Can I get something for you?"

"From up thar? Oh, I don't need nothin'."

"Chocolate?"

He smiled. "Chocklit would be nice."

Walking back to the truck, I thought about why Jimmy had loved him so much. June was innocent. He was hidden away from the world. He knew everything he needed to know, and because of that, he never worried about a thing.

I wondered what it was like not to want more. I held it against the kids in Covington that they didn't aspire to anything beyond what they had. But I admired June's satisfaction with his quiet little life in the hollow.

June knew a side of Jimmy that no one else did but me. One time, June broke his hip falling out of an apple tree, and his sister had to push him into town in a wheelbarrow. Jimmy saw them coming down the road and drove them to the hospital, where June had to stay for three weeks.

Jimmy was worried that being in a hospital so long would kill June. I was standing by June's hospital bed when Jimmy said to him, "How are you going to lie here for three weeks?"

June smiled. "I reckon I just will. Then there will be a day when it's time to go home."

THIRTY-FOUR

THURSDAY NIGHT WAYNE and I stayed up and loaded the trailer. Tack, brushes, braiding supplies, buckets, extra hay nets, feed, blankets, leg wraps, shipping boots, muscle rubs, a salt block, vet supplies, extra shoes, extra bits and tack.

Before I went to sleep, I opened *Hunter Seat Equitation* and read a few pages at random.

> Once definite controls and an established position have been set at home, the rider is free to concentrate on getting his horse to perform well at a show.

George was right, except he was assuming he was talking to a normal kid with a normal horse. A kid who was following a training program with a real trainer and taking lessons four times a week on a made horse, not a rider who had pulled a gun on a crazy man in her own house just a couple of days earlier. Not a horse that had to show his ability by jumping over four feet of barbed wire and rotting boards.

> It is much too late to worry about form while in a class.

It's never too late to worry about anything, I thought.

> Riding well is all that counts, and if faults are spotted, they must be put off as homework for the next week. One has enough to think of in controlling his horse's pace, smooth transitions, riding proper lines and turns, and getting his fences. The very worst thing an instructor can do to a rider before entering the ring is to clutter his mind. It just makes matters worse.

If he only knew how cluttered my mind was already.

Friday morning we got up at five. Wayne made us breakfast while I wrapped Sonny's legs and fed him hay. I didn't give him grain because I didn't want him to colic on the road.

"You got hoof polish? Mineral oil?" Wayne asked. Wayne had replaced his belt buckle with a shiny new one.

I nodded.

Wayne got in and started the truck. I got in and closed

the door. Melinda was still asleep and I hadn't wanted to wake her up, but when I turned, she was standing by the truck window in her bathrobe. "Call me when you get there."

"Okay." I lowered my voice. "Let the cat inside."

She nodded and smiled. It was nice to be on the same side as her again.

"You be careful," she said to Wayne.

"Bye, Mama," I said. I hadn't called her that in a long time.

"Bye, honey." She kissed me on the forehead.

I looked back at the farm, but it was too dark to see anything. We were rolling, and Wayne shifted gears slowly as the truck powered up. A few moments later, Sonny started stomping and slamming around in the trailer.

"What in the devil . . ." Wayne said.

The trailer shook hard and Wayne grabbed the steering wheel. He slowed down and looked at the side-view mirror.

"What's his problem?" I asked.

"He misses his buddy," Wayne said.

"We gotta bring Sub."

"Damn it all!" he said.

He pushed down on the brake and the horse kept pawing loudly. We made a U-turn through a gas station.

Chester, one of Wayne's old buddies, was filling his tank. "Y'all goin' up to New York City?"

"We sure are," said Wayne.

Chester laughed. "Y'all are crazy."

Once we were facing home, the horse stopped pawing. When we pulled in, Sub was standing at the fence, calling loudly to Sonny, who called back and stomped in the trailer. Mama was at the window shaking her head.

"Pathetic," Wayne said, looking at Submarine. "I ain't heard that horse make a sound in years."

I put up a hay net for Sub, and Wayne walked him to the back of the trailer. He hopped right in.

I thought about Kelly and her team of grooms. I bet they were loading her horses into a rig with a camera on every horse and monitors in the front. On second thought, Kelly was probably flying and meeting the horses there.

We drove through the winding roads of Bath County with the mist rising off the fields, up and over Warm Springs Mountain, through Goshen, past Craigsville, through the hilly streets of Staunton. Then we climbed onto Route 81 and powered up, getting in line with the tractor-trailers heading north.

We listened to the radio without talking.

After about half an hour, Wayne asked me if I was nervous.

"No," I lied. "I just hope luck is on our side."

"Sidney, if you work hard, day after day, you create your own luck. Thomas Jefferson said, 'I'm a great believer in luck, and I find the harder I work, the more I have of it.'"

"He didn't say that."

"He sure as hell did."

"You got that off a coffee mug at White's Truck Stop."

"Look it up. He said it."

"Then what's your excuse?" I challenged him. "You seem like one unlucky old bastard."

"I ain't talking about me. I'm talking about you."

We stopped in Winchester to check on the horses. We gave them some water and got back on the road. The sun was bright, and Wayne put on his sunglasses.

"Can you see through those things?" I asked him. "They look pretty dirty." He handed them to me. I wiped them off with a paper napkin and gave them back to him.

We passed into West Virginia, then Maryland right after that, and I realized I had never been this far north.

"I was riding to Covington with old Curtis — you know, Curtis who lives behind the piggery, works down at the mill, Joe's son?"

I shrugged, not sure. I just wanted to listen. Wayne only told stories when he was relaxed, and that made me feel better.

"Curtis, he wears glasses, and he had his license picture taken with them glasses on. So we was going to Covington and there was this roadblock up, and Curtis said, 'Daggone it, I don't have my glasses on. I'm going to get a ticket. I got my glasses on in my license picture. Hand me your'n,' he said.

So he put on these glasses I had in the truck with no lenses in 'em."

I started laughing at the thought of Wayne's old friend wearing glasses with no lenses in them.

"So when we got to the roadblock, we stopped directly, and Curtis, he just looked straight ahead, and the deputy just looked at his license and looked at him and said, 'Mr. Curtis, I s'pose you better get some lenses for those glasses.' And Curtis said, 'Oh my God, they done fell out of my frames,' he said. 'I can't believe it!'

"Ha!" Wayne laughed so hard that he shook. "Ha! 'They done fell out of my frames. I can't believe it!'"

When he stopped laughing, I started, and then we just kept cracking up.

Right about when I realized I had six hours to do exactly nothing, whatever I wanted, anything, or all three, Wayne told me to do my homework. I shrugged it off and he snapped at me. "Girl, you do your damn homework or you ain't riding."

"Ha! You're telling me I ain't riding?" I said.

"You heard me. All that time you spend fighting about your homework, not doing it, explaining why you didn't do it — well, you could have done it five times by then."

Shit, I thought, *he's right.* I thought about pointing out that he hadn't gotten past the eighth grade, but that would have been stupid for a lot of reasons, and he had a mean-enough look in his eye that I didn't want to fight about it. I opened up my biology book and started reading about plankton. I gnawed on my fingernails and shifted around in my seat, doing anything I could to avoid thinking about that God-awful boring book, but then I imagined having it all done. So I read it, and by the time we were in Harrisburg, Pennsylvania, I had answered the last question and slammed the book shut.

The signs looked dirty, and the reflective pavement markers were battered, unlike the perfectly uniform reflectors on Afton Mountain. We drove along right next to a concrete barrier that shifted left and right to avoid construction. It made me nervous as hell. Wayne had both hands on the wheel, and his face had gotten tight. The shoulder of the highway was strewn with litter, a towel, a CD, food wrappers. It looked chaotic and a little wild, like it was every man for himself.

When the highway straightened out again, I relaxed and fell asleep. I woke up when we were pulling in at a truck stop in New Jersey. We left the horses and went inside for lunch, sitting where we could see them. I drank a Coke and used the bathroom. The people looked different from the ones at home. They had dark hair and looked a little harder, a little tougher on the outside, and they sure were in a hurry. They spoke fast and didn't look you in the eye.

Finally, we saw the twinkling lights of New York City. I could not believe how beautiful and scary it was or that people lived and worked and ate and slept on that island. We'd lost the country station on the radio, and now we were getting music I'd never heard before. I felt chills going up and down my arms. It seemed crazy to bring these silly horses into this big city. I was so excited, I wanted to cry. I couldn't look at Wayne.

I saw the Empire State Building in the distance, and it seemed both frightening and encouraging, like it was there for me. One of the horses stomped hard, like he knew something was happening.

I looked down at my lap. My hands were clenching the map and shaking. Wayne was chomping on a toothpick so hard, I thought he might swallow it.

"Yep, there she is," he said. His voice sounded different than usual. His throat was tight. He must have been excited and nervous, too. I asked him what the buildings were for.

"I guess some of those are people houses," he said. "Offices. You know." City people were like bees in a beehive. I couldn't imagine.

We lined up at the Holland Tunnel. The people in the cars looked bored. A couple of them cut in front of us, but then a shiny black Lincoln waved us in. I was glued to the window, thrilled and terrified.

We were getting ready to go through when I saw a sign up ahead: TRAILERS PROHIBITED.

"Shit," Wayne said.

We were in a lane with no tollgate. He hit the gas, we blew through some kind of sensor, we heard somebody yell, and we went down into the tunnel.

Here we were, under a great river, in a tube of concrete and steel, with Submarine and Sonny. The yellow lights passed rhythmically across Wayne's face.

We came out about five minutes later — not soon enough — into a cloverleaf of cars and signs and construction. There was a police car behind us and Wayne pulled over, but everybody started honking and the car went past us.

"What in God's name . . ." Wayne muttered.

I concentrated on the map. "This West Side Highway will take you up to Thirty-Fourth Street, and that will take you to Madison Square Garden."

He followed my directions to the West Side Highway. There were thousands of cars all jammed up next to each other, honking their horns. I was so glad not to be driving. I saw beautiful glass buildings that looked like mirrored pirate ships, a crazy cement building straddling a train track with plants and trees growing out of it, and cars, cars, cars, streaming everywhere. I rolled down my window and heard honking, music, laughter. Wayne clamped down on a new toothpick just as a helicopter landed right outside his damn window.

I just laughed. A helicopter! Landing right by the water!

"Good God Almighty, let's just hope the horses don't see that!" he yelled.

We turned onto Thirty-Fourth Street. People were honking at us, and I rolled my window up and slouched down. Wayne made a turn onto a street and then realized it was one-way and started to back up. He was getting tense as hell.

A driver yelled something at him that I couldn't hear.

"Well, to hell with you, too — I got two horses in here!" Wayne said. Then he sighed and slumped down like he was at the end of his rope.

We circled around, passing the Empire State Building. I couldn't see the top, but the doors on that building were beautiful. Wayne stepped on the gas, forced his way through an opening, and finally got us to Madison Square Garden — but we were on the wrong side. He swore, and we waited at a light to circle around the block.

I saw a lady in nice clothes eating a slice of pizza while she was waiting to cross the street. I wondered why she didn't have time to sit somewhere and finish it. I saw people of all different colors going home from work, all standing right next to each other. They looked like blood cells being pumped through the arteries, stopping at the lights between heartbeats. I looked into the side-view mirror and saw Sonny's nose sticking out between the slats of the trailer, snorting. He was sucking in the air, the car fumes, the steam rising up from the sewers — breathing in coffee, food, perfume. I was smelling all that myself.

Damned if the four of us weren't already exhausted.

THIRTY-FIVE

We turned into an underground garage and a man waved us in. We drove down through a tunnel and into a makeshift stable area. Horses were being walked around, sweaty from traveling. Boy, it was tight down there. We parked where they told us to, and an official checked us in. I watched Wayne count out a lot of cash.

The official looked into the trailer. "You're only down for one horse," he said with an accent I had only heard on TV.

"Our horse brought his assistant," I said.

"No room for two horses." Wow. Just like that. He said it pretty mean.

I begged him. "They have to be together. Please."

"Honey, there's no room."

Wayne was thinking.

"You know Seabiscuit?" Wayne asked.

"Sure," the man said.

"He traveled with a pony. They cut a hole between their stalls so they could see each other."

"I thought he had a goat," said the man.

"They started with a goat, but Seabiscuit picked the goat up and tossed him out when the goat tried to eat his food."

"This ain't Seabiscuit," the man said.

"This is our Seabiscuit, fella," Wayne said.

"Then they have to share a stall, and the stalls aren't big enough."

We parked the trailer in a tiny underground garage area with low ceilings and unloaded the horses.

The official was right. The stalls really were too small for two horses. We tied Sub up in front of Sonny until we could figure out what to do.

Once we'd unloaded the trailer and stacked the equipment next to the stall, Wayne had to go out and park a few blocks away. I wished him luck, and he just shook his head and got into the truck.

"See if you can't change that fella's mind," he said, pushing three crisp twenties into my hand.

I went out and found the stall man. "Sir, I know what the rules are, and I'm sorry, but I don't know what to do. My uncle said you might be able to rent us another stall." I handed him the money like it was nothing, and he took it. He nodded for me to follow him and pointed to an empty stall around the corner. I put Sub in there. Sonny and Sub couldn't see each other, and they started calling back and forth.

"You ain't cutting holes in any walls," the man said.

Wayne came back with our bags from the truck and said we needed to check in at the hotel.

The hotel was just a rundown building with fire escapes zigzagging across the front. Trucks roared by and banged over metal plates in the street so loudly that I jumped every time. A group of men were hanging out in front of a dirty little store on the corner with bright yellow lights and newspapers. Some men were black and some looked Spanish. They didn't pay any attention to us when we walked by.

Inside the hotel, a big lady in a purple sweatshirt checked us in and didn't so much as say hello. I wondered how on earth I would ever fall asleep there, and I wished I had my .44.

"I'm not sharing a room with you — you snore like a chain saw," I said.

"Then find another one. I think there's a vacancy at the Four Seasons," Wayne said.

He opened the door to our room. It was tiny and musty, right above the dirty little store, and it smelled like an ashtray. I looked at the room, looked out the window. Wayne stared out at a bar across the avenue, the sign blinking.

"Don't even think about it," I said.

"You either," he joked.

Wayne sat down on one of the beds. "Room's so small you can't cuss a cat without getting hair in your mouth," he said, taking off his boots. He lay down, and before I knew it, he was snoring loudly.

I called Melinda and told her we were there. I made her promise to call Earl if Donald showed up, but we didn't think he would. Setting foot on Wayne's property would be a capital offense in Wayne's neck of the woods, and Donald knew it.

I changed into my pajamas, then lay down on the other bed with the George Morris equitation book, but I couldn't concentrate. For some reason, I started thinking about God. I asked him to watch out for me, and I started to cry, even though I wasn't sad or anything. I didn't even know if I believed in God, but if he or she was out there, I could have used some help.

Even with millions of people, New York was lonely in the middle of the night.

I got up, put my clothes back on, and walked out of the room. I went outside and walked down Ninth Avenue all by myself. People moved fast. When I looked at them, they looked back at me. When I didn't look, I didn't think they did, either. A lot of people were short and had dark hair, and I wasn't used to seeing so many black people. They seemed different from the black people at home — confident, like their being black wasn't a problem for them or for anybody else.

I was at the Garden in ten minutes. It didn't feel strange to me now because I knew Sonny and Sub were there.

Three trainers were riding horses in the warm-up ring,

and I had to show some papers to get past the guard. Sonny was sleeping crouched down in the shavings like a dog. Sub was asleep on his side, legs out, snoring like a big old pig. He couldn't have cared less. I went back to Sonny's stall, spread out one of his blankets along the wall on top of the shavings, lay down, and fell asleep.

THIRTY-SIX

NEXT THING I knew, Wayne threw open the metal stall door with a loud bang, scaring the devil out of me. Sonny was standing up, eating hay.

Wayne stared at me, his face tight and worried.

"You knew where I'd be," I croaked.

"No, I didn't know where you'd be!" he roared. "Nearly had a heart attack!"

"I'm sorry."

He checked Sonny's legs and ran his hand along Sonny's body to make sure he hadn't rubbed into anything during the night. Sometimes that happened in a show stall. Sonny still had shavings all over him, even on the top of his back, from a hard night's sleep.

"Get a saddle on him," Wayne said.

I looked at my watch. 6:03 a.m. I threw the tack on, put on my helmet, tightened Sonny's girth, and stuck my left foot into the stirrup. I felt a sharp pain in my knee. My legs were tight from sitting in the truck for ten hours the day before. I tried again and pushed through the pain.

We brought Sonny into the tiny warm-up ring, where about six horses were being schooled. A man stopped us and asked for our official warm-up time. I didn't know what he was talking about.

"You mean to tell me we have to sign up to school the damn horse?" Wayne said.

The man looked at his clipboard, flipped through some papers. "We're full."

Full?

"But I might have a spot . . ."

I let out my breath.

"Three o'clock tomorrow morning."

"You gotta be kidding me!" said Wayne.

"That's all we got."

That poor horse wasn't going to know what hit him when I tacked him up at two thirty in the morning. He'd probably sleepwalk through the whole thing and kill us both.

The official started talking to someone else, and we decided to let the horse look around.

That was when I really started worrying.

The schooling area was about a third the size of a normal one, with metal columns that the riders had to maneuver around. It was plain crazy to ride a horse in a place like that. And the worst part was the noise — every time a horse whinnied, the sound bounced around so you didn't know where it was coming from.

Sonny was jigging on and off and not responding to my legs. I patted him behind the saddle and on the neck and told him it was okay. Then I sat up and tried to get him forward on the bit, but it only made him jig harder.

"Easy," I said, trying to sound calm. But I sounded shaken up, and I was.

The horse was as tight as a drum, and there was no place to ride him down, no field to turn him out in. He felt like he was about to explode, and my mind jumped around, trying to come up with a way to make him feel better. If we were at home, I'd take him for a ride in the woods. Not here.

A trainer was watching from the side of the ring. "Is this the first time he's been to a show?" he said.

The trainer looked like a mannequin in a department store. His collar was crisply folded over his down vest. His jeans were clean and pressed. His dark brown paddock boots didn't have even a scuff on the toe.

I didn't know what to say to him. He probably wasn't asking because he cared. It seemed as though everywhere I looked, people were sizing me up.

"Put him back in his stall," said Wayne, ignoring the trainer. "He needs to quiet down and get used to the place. Just give him some hay and leave him alone today."

"The show starts tomorrow!"

"You can't ride him until three o'clock in the morning, honey." He yawned.

"People are looking at us," I said.

"Screw them," he said, and he meant it.

Sometimes I loved that nasty old man.

"I'm going back to get some rest," he said. "Didn't sleep a wink all night, with those people jabbering outside."

That was the beginning of the day before the championship: the longest day of my life.

THIRTY-SEVEN

I put Sonny back in his stall and hung up his tack. He was looking at everything, pacing, wearing a ditch in the shavings. He ignored his hay, stuck his head over the door, raised his nose, and sniffed the air, trying to smell the other horses. He was a herd animal stuck in a box underground, a nightmare for him. The other horses had spent years learning how to do this, accompanying seasoned horses to shows, slowly building up to it. But not Sonny. I decided to leave him alone.

In the next stall was a beautiful chestnut gelding with big eyes. Two girls were taking pictures of him, feeding him snacks, and sweet-talking him. One girl, the chatty one, was tall and had long curly brown hair; the other one was little and quiet, with a tight blond ponytail and bright eyes.

"He'll eat anything. Watch this," said the chatty one to the other. She gave the horse a granola bar, and he took it in his mouth and chewed. A wave of drool spilled out the sides.

They laughed. The horse nodded for more.

"I can't wait until we go to Florida."

"When's the first show?"

"I'll ask my mom."

The chestnut horse kept nodding for food, and the girls stroked his face.

"Ernie, you are so silly," the taller one gushed.

I wasn't used to seeing people enjoy themselves like this at a show, not after all the time I'd spent around Kelly.

The brown-haired girl hugged the horse around the neck while he chewed. "I want to keep him forever," she said.

It had to be one of those hundred-thousand-dollar lease horses.

"Will you braid my hair?" she asked her friend.

"Sure."

The blond one hopped up onto a step stool and started combing the other one's hair.

"Use the purple yarn to match Ernie's braids."

"Okay!"

I stood there by Sonny's stall watching them. They weren't like the girls at Oak Hill. These girls seemed carefree and happy, as if nothing in the world mattered.

I walked over to the arena. *I'm in Madison Square Garden,* I told myself. There were flags from other countries hanging down, and there were electronic letters on a ticker floating by underneath them: "ASPCA MACLAY FINALS," over and over.

I sat in the stands. It was nine o'clock in the morning, and there were about two dozen other people sitting in the seats while the crew dragged the arena, smoothing it out and getting ready to start building the course.

I saw one girl standing by the in-gate nervously tapping her foot. A man who I guessed was her father walked over to her, and she snapped at him to leave her alone.

Two women sat down in front of me. They were pretty, with nice sweaters, jewelry, and clean dark blue jeans.

"I know four girls applying for a spot in the ninth grade," said one.

"How many of them are Greystone material?"

"Seriously."

"When you talk to that admissions person, show total respect. Whatever it takes. Cry if you have to. Beg."

"Whatever it takes," the other agreed.

"You know what they say — if you don't want to play by the rules, don't play."

"Of course. We're playing."

"And then the girls will be in the same class!"

"Knock on wood."

"Knock on wood."

"I don't know what I'll do if she has to go to public school."

She turned and caught me looking at her. Very quickly, her eyes moved from my face down to my feet and then away.

Something told me these ladies weren't there because they loved horses.

I left and walked through the stable area. Grooms were washing, feeding, cleaning stalls, soaking and wrapping legs, clipping. Hardly any riders in sight. A big black horse leaned on his canvas webbing and pawed loudly on the concrete. His groom whistled and swept along, swatting the horse's feet out of the aisle.

I saw a sticker on a tack trunk that said "Live your dreams." Everywhere I looked these days, I saw stickers and mugs and posters that told people to live their dreams, as if the only way to be alive was to go for it. That was true if you didn't fail. If you failed, people thought you were a fool. I wondered if the people who said to live your dreams were going to pay my rent when living my dreams didn't work out.

I looked at the groom sweeping and whistling. I had more in common with him than with those ladies talking by the ring, and it wasn't because they had money. They thought they were winning at a game that the rest of us were losing. This groom sweeping the floor in a neat pattern, getting his work done early, loving his job — he wasn't losing anything. He was playing a different game.

I was waiting for the officials to post the course and the "order of go." Then I'd know how much time I had to braid. If I braided today, the day before, Sonny might rub the braids out. And somehow I had to find time to sleep, because my schooling time was at three o'clock in the morning.

When I went back to the stalls, there was Sub, standing loose in the aisle, eating hay. He could have run out the damn doors and right down Thirty-Fourth Street if he'd wanted to. One of the girls I'd been watching before, the one with dark hair, was putting a halter on him.

"He's an escape artist!" she said when she saw me coming. "I'm Caroline," she said, patting Sub. "And this is Laura."

"Hi. I'm Sid."

We smiled at each other, and I put Sub back in his stall. This time I clipped all three snaps of the webbing to the eye-hooks so he wouldn't get out.

"He's sweet."

"Yeah."

"Did you bring him for company?" Caroline asked.

I nodded. "Is that your horse?" I asked, pointing at the chestnut.

"I borrowed him from a lady I ride for," she said. "Just for the show. Dollar lease. I can't afford an eq horse." She smiled a little and shrugged. I didn't realize kids at this level dollar-leased, too.

"I did that once," I said, thinking about Ruby, although I'd never given Beezie a dollar and we'd never written up a lease. We'd just put a halter on Ruby and loaded her up.

Caroline gestured toward Sonny. "Is he your horse?" she asked.

"My uncle's," I said.

"He's cute. A little nervous, but he'll settle down," Laura said.

"Yeah," I said. "You guys don't seem nervous."

"Oh, we're freaking out. But what can you do?" she said. "You come here, you ride, you try not to kill yourself, and you go home and get ready for the next show."

I had always thought I'd never make friends with girls who showed horses. They were usually all kinds of mean and snobby. But girls like these two could be my friends. They were happy. I didn't think you were allowed to be happy until you were at least twenty-two.

A trainer appeared, and she seemed in a hurry. I'd seen her in *Practical Horseman* but I didn't know her name. She was big and round with a long blond braid — preppy, with an alligator on her shirt and a pink leather belt with gold shells that connected in the middle.

She stopped in front of Caroline and Laura and took a dramatic breath.

"Girls, they posted the course."

The girls followed her down the aisle.

I couldn't move.

Laura turned around and waved for me to join them. "Come on!" she said, and I did.

Near the ring, coaches and riders were gathered around a bulletin board. Right in front of it was Wayne.

Before I could get over to him, I heard Wes's voice. "Sid, you drew second."

I turned around, so glad to see him. "Hi!" I said. "When is your schooling time? Where are your stalls?"

Kelly came up next to him. "Hi, Sid," she said. "You hear what Wes said?"

My brain was frozen.

"You're second," she said.

I was going second. Out of two hundred.

Wes grabbed me by the elbow and pulled me toward Wayne. "Go look at the course."

Wayne was rubbing his whiskers and looking at the course diagram, his brow wrinkled. I wanted to see but there were riders in my way. I finally squeezed through and tried to concentrate on the course.

It started with an oxer, then a hard turn to a skinny vertical. Then a tight 270-degree turn to an in-and-out. Then a rollback to an airy fan jump, then a combination of three fences: oxer, vertical, oxer. Then a deep turn into the corner, and the killer: a combination of two fences so close to the corner of the ring that they would seem to pop up out of nowhere to the horse and rider on course. Finally, for the eleventh and twelfth jumps, a right-angle turn coming off the tenth to another airy vertical, and a complete 180-degree turn before a hard right into the final fence, a big wall.

I heard a girl suck in her breath as she studied the

diagram. "It's okay, honey—everyone has to do the same course," her mom said.

The ring crew was putting up the jumps in front of us. The fences looked huge.

Dutch dismounted and talked intently to Kelly, pointing at the course. I couldn't hear what he was saying, but I could see him gesturing for her to ride forward, ride strong. Then I heard him say the word *bold.*

"Riders, you may walk the course," said the announcer.

The trainers got in there first, and their riders fell into line behind them. The trainers reminded me of generals storming a battlefield. They took long, confident strides in their black leather boots as they walked, fence by fence.

Wayne and I walked the course side by side. "One fence at a time, honey, one fence at a time," he said.

We counted strides. I had never done this seriously before. I usually just used my eye to pick a takeoff spot. We started at the base of the fence and took two normal steps. That was for landing. Then we took long steps toward the next fence, three of our steps equaling one of Sonny's. Then the last two normal steps were for takeoff. I could hear coaches and riders debating the length of each line. Boy, was this complicated.

Sonny had a big stride, but not enormous. He could play things long, like pull a five-stride distance into four, but I could also get five strides out of him. That meant I needed to use my eye and not count too much. As if reading my mind, Wayne said, "Use your eye. No counting in the ring." I nodded. We counted only to figure out if we needed to collect our horses or lengthen their strides.

"Riders, please leave the ring," the announcer said.

"You need to sleep," Wayne said.

As if I could.

We checked the horses, and then Wayne walked me back to the hotel. When we got to our room, Wayne turned on the television, and I lay down and passed out until two o'clock in the morning.

THIRTY-EIGHT

"Ride him down, just ride him down," Wayne said.

I'd need a ring the size of a racetrack to ride him down. Sonny had tried to bolt when I tacked him up and got on, a little before three o'clock. I stayed off his back and let him trot around as fast as he wanted. When he pulled on my arms, I let him have as much rein as I could so he wouldn't start fighting me. Now he was looking at everything, everywhere. His back was so tight, I was afraid he'd pull something. I felt trapped in that underground cave with a crazy horse and no relief in sight. The biggest competition of my life.

We entered the ring with a bunch of other kids who were stuck schooling at three o'clock in the morning. Their horses looked fine. Sonny's head was high and he was about to pull my arms off.

After a few minutes, Wayne saw that it wasn't working. He grabbed Sonny tightly by the reins, under the chin. He walked us out of the ring toward the exit to the street, where the trailers had come in.

"Sir! No horses allowed over there!" said a security guard. Wayne ignored him.

"Where are you going?" I asked.

"Just do what I tell you," Wayne said.

He walked us outside onto Eighth Avenue, holding Sonny's cheek piece tightly in his big hand. Sonny was snorting and looking around.

"Someone explain to me how a horse who used to show on the A-circuit is acting like this," I said to him.

"Because this horse ain't really been showed. On any circuit."

I felt like he'd punched me in the stomach. "What do you mean, he ain't been showed?" I yelled.

"He was in the killing pen. At the Front Royal Auction."

It had to be a joke. I looked at Wayne's face, but he was dead serious. He was putting his cards on the table because he didn't know what the hell else to do.

I'd never seen him before when he didn't know what to do, and I didn't like it one bit.

"You brought me up here, to New York City, to ride a horse from the *killing pen?*" I asked him, not really expecting an answer.

"You brought yourself up here."

Now I was furious. "You're a damn liar."

"Chew-Gum lied to me."

"What a surprise! Chew-Gum lied!"

We walked down the sidewalk, the horse's shoes scraping on the concrete. I listened to the metal clinks of his shoes, making sure they were all the same pitch, a habit I couldn't help, even now. If one of them had a high pitch, it most likely meant a loose shoe. Sonny's shoes sounded okay.

Wayne led us over a metal grate in the sidewalk, and Sonny nearly jumped out of his skin.

"Whoa, now! Easy," Wayne said, pulling him back onto the sidewalk. People were walking around us, afraid of the horse, as they damn well should have been. He was so worked up, he could've stomped anyone, Wayne and me included.

"When'd you find this out?" I asked Wayne. "That he was in the killing pen?"

"I called to get his show record. Nobody could find it, so I called Chew-Gum and he told me the truth." Keeping his eyes on Sonny, Wayne mumbled under his breath, "He's a shit liar. Once you lie, you stick to it."

"I'm going to make a fool out of myself, if I don't break my neck."

Wayne was as scared as I was. He had as much at stake as I did. But he was in even deeper shit. On top of everything, he was responsible for me, and I was just a kid. I would have felt sorry for him if I hadn't wanted to wring his neck for not telling me the truth.

We'd walked a block, and Sonny was jogging along like a racehorse heading to the gate. But he was starting to wind down, just a little. We passed a pair of carriage horses pulling an empty buckboard. The driver had on a tuxedo with a rose in the lapel and a black top hat. His dapple gray Percherons were matched to the teeth and trotting in perfect step.

"You let me down, you'll be pulling a cart, too," I grumbled at Sonny.

A couple of men were playing jazz music on the corner. Wayne pulled Sonny right up to them, and the trumpet player turned and bleated a note in his direction. I thought that damn horse would climb up a tree, but he just shivered, then took a long, deep breath and blew it out loudly with a snort.

"It's about time," said Wayne. "Crazy son of a bitch."

"Good boy," I said, patting Sonny's neck with one hand, holding his reins tightly with the other.

Wayne let go of the bridle and fastened a long lead shank onto the bit. We walked back to the arena, both of us a little relieved.

Our scheduled warm-up time was over, but the lady let us into the ring for twenty minutes. We trotted a pole, about two feet six inches high. Wayne raised it higher, and we doubled back and trotted it again. The ring was so tight that I thought I might jump right out by accident, and we weren't even cantering yet. Sonny was a little less hot but still not listening to me.

Wayne set up a higher pole, and we cantered it, pulling a rail that banged loudly. A couple of people turned and looked.

"He's not paying attention," I said to Wayne.

"Let's make him pay attention," Wayne said. He set up a high jump, about three feet nine inches — a big oxer. I shook my head.

"Girl." Wayne tightened his mouth like he was mad. "That horse can get over this jump and you know it."

"He can also crash right through it," I said.

"Get over here," he said, jerking his head at me in a way he hadn't done in a while. When I went over to him, I realized he looked pale and worn out. "If you're already talking like that, then forget it."

I looked around at all the people watching.

"Since when do you care so much what other people think?" he asked.

"I wish I didn't."

"Then don't! Who gives a damn if the horse runs through that fence?" He waited for a response, but I didn't answer.

"Huh?" he demanded.

"Just me and you," I said. "We're the ones who care."

"That's right. And deep down, do we really give a damn?" He was looking right at me. I thought of his icy blue eyes staring down at me when I'd fallen off the red horse in the rain.

"No." I was surprised, but I meant it. Deep, deep down, I really didn't care.

I thought about the people I admired, like Eileen Cleek, like George Morris, like Beezie Winants. My father. And Wayne. They didn't give a royal shit what anyone thought about them.

What had happened to me, that I suddenly cared so much how people looked at me? As a little kid, I'd walk into the supermarket with dirt in my hair, and I didn't give a goddamn if someone thought I was living in a car. But being in ninth grade, and going to Oak Hill, and being around people like Dee Dee and Kelly, I'd started feeling their eyes on me and wondering if they were right about me, that they were better than me.

I had to take turns with another girl over that big fence Wayne had built. She looked fantastic. Then she dismounted and a different girl got on, trotting around in a figure eight. I realized the first one was her trainer.

"See," said the trainer, "she's bending better to the left."

"Thanks," said the girl.

I couldn't imagine Wayne getting on and riding for me. He knew he couldn't do a better job than I could.

"Do you want to catch a bigger oxer in here?" the trainer asked the girl. She nodded yes, they built my oxer into a bigger one, and her horse went over it like a Grand Prix jumper.

Wayne lowered the fence back to three feet three inches. I cantered the biggest circle I could, feeling a little wobbly. Then I pretended I was twelve and I was jumping some crazy pony, not caring what anyone thought. Not worrying, not thinking of all the things that could go wrong. Just imagining it working.

Sonny got in deep and jumped it, ears straight forward as though he were saying to himself, *Damn, she's serious.* We were still in the air when I heard Wayne yell, "Good!" We landed, and Sonny dropped his head, got behind the bit, and thought about bucking but didn't. He was happy. I wondered who was a bigger mental case, him or me.

Wayne checked his watch. "We gotta get him braided," he said.

We walked out of the ring. I dismounted, and we led the horse through the dark aisles.

I untacked Sonny and put him into his stall. Wayne grabbed a stool, and I got the braiding kit, hopped onto the stool, and started dividing his mane into sections. Wayne wiped off the tack, then fed and hayed both horses.

It was five o'clock.

Wes appeared in the doorway.

"You start on the tail, I'll do the mane," he said.

"Aren't you braiding for Kelly?"

"She's going forty-fifth."

He was concerned because I was going second. That made me feel flattered and insanely nervous at the same time.

"You scared?" Wes asked.

"Why?"

"You ain't said a word."

"I'm so nervous, I feel like I'm in a bad dream."

"Use it," he said.

I wasn't sure I could. The biggest problem now wasn't the horse or the ring, it was me.

We braided for an hour, listening to the Spanish music from the grooms' radio. My mind raced. Wayne went to the snack bar and got some water and a muffin for me. I picked at it, but I couldn't eat.

Wes had done a perfect job braiding the mane and rebraided the tail for me. It looked beautiful.

It was time to go.

Sonny had decided to lie down in the stall and was covered in shavings. I wiped him off and tacked him up.

Wayne gave me a leg up and walked with me to the warm-up ring. I let Sonny walk on a loose rein and look around.

And then I spotted Edgar. Wearing the biggest grin I'd ever seen, his face shining from sweat, he ran over to me. His eyes welled with tears.

"Very nice," he said, looking Sonny and me up and down, straightening Sonny's noseband.

"I'm okay?" I asked him, knowing he had the last word.

"You're great," he said.

"In about two minutes, we'll begin the first round of the ASPCA Maclay Finals," the announcer boomed through the warm-up area. "On deck is number one hundred seventy-one, then seventy-two . . ."

That was me.

Wayne grabbed the reins under Sonny's chin. Edgar pulled the rub rag off his shoulder and chased after us, shining my boots and wiping off Sonny's legs.

Kelly was bickering with her mother near the ring. She saw me looking, and she walked over to me. I thought she was going to wish me luck, but no.

"Sid, I have to tell you — I'm only telling you this to help you, because you're not really used to the show circuit . . ." Her tone was snotty and knowing — the usual.

I braced myself, wanting to know what snide thing she had to say, ready to take the punishment, thinking I deserved it. But then I thought about Sonny and Wayne, and how hard we'd worked, and how letting her into my mind could ruin all of it. Whatever she said would stay with me. It would be the gift that kept on giving, forever.

I turned, looked her right in the eye, and said very calmly, "I don't care. Whatever it is, I don't want to hear it."

She recoiled. "Oh my God, I just —"

"Good luck. I hope you have a great round. I love that horse," I said.

I gathered up Sonny's reins and walked away from her. I wondered what on earth I'd done to some people to make them act like that. Maybe the real question I needed to answer was why I cared what she thought anyway.

Sonny was still looking around. A flash photo. A girl playing with a ribbon. A man taking off his jacket too quickly.

"Now I see why you did this drunk," I said to Wayne.

"You know it," he said.

"Sonny needs something to occupy his mind."

"He's about to get something," Wayne answered. "Sidney . . ." Then his face got serious and he reached into his jacket. He pulled out a faded velvet jewelry box, opened it, and held up a simple gold stock pin. "Your grandma wore it. It was hers."

"Thanks, Wayne."

I took the box from him and picked up the pin. The cold metal felt good in my hand. My grandmother. I felt like she was there, on my team. I put the pin into my collar.

"First up is number one seventy-one, Justin Burke from Greenwich, Connecticut," boomed the announcer.

We watched Justin do the course. He made a few errors, but because he was the first one to go, it would count a little less against him.

"On course is number seventy-two, Sidney Criser from Covington, Virginia." It sounded as though he was talking about someone else until he said "Covington." I bet the name Covington had never boomed across Madison Square Garden before.

I entered the ring and we picked up a trot. Sonny looked into the stands, seeing them for the first time. I pushed him on and circled, lining up the first fence.

Like Wayne had said, I could only jump one fence at a time and not the whole damn course, so that was what I was going to do. Every fence demanded a different approach — a forward ride, a collected ride, a light hand, a heavy hand. A couple of times I let Sonny land and gather himself up at his own pace; other times I never lost contact with his mouth and got him right into the next fence. Twelve fences. One at a time. Forward, bold, no counting.

I saw Wayne watching, still as a statue.

I got a little tense, and Sonny sped up. I remembered to keep my eyes soft and to take it all in — not to stare a hole through the jump. Sonny settled as soon as I made the adjustment.

We were supposed to gallop down to the final fence, and boy, did we. I heard Wayne say, "Whoa," and I steadied Sonny just a bit before we took the last jump. We landed. First round over.

Pretty damn good.

I heard loud clapping and looked over at Wayne, but his hands were still gripping the rail. It was Wes, Edgar, and even Martha and Herbert Wakefield. And strangers. Strangers were clapping for me.

Coming out of the ring, I was giddy. I'd done it. It wasn't a disaster.

Wayne walked toward me with a spring in his step. "Not bad. Not bad a-tall."

"Thanks. You see him look at that fan jump? You see him race down that line?"

He laughed. "I sure did. But he did it." He patted the horse's neck, and we walked away from the arena.

Now there were one hundred and ninety-eight riders to go, and I had to wait three hours before I'd know what was next.

THIRTY-NINE

I PUT SONNY INTO his stall, pulled his saddle off, and unhooked the throat latch. His face was already in his hay before I got the bit out of his mouth. He was acting like a horse again and not some kind of crazy monkey. I filled his water bucket, took off my helmet, and tried to rest.

Wayne brought over a cardboard tray with sandwiches and handed it to me, scowling. "Fourteen goddamn dollars."

We sat in the stands, watching the riders go. They were from all over the country. Santa Cruz, California. Princeton, New Jersey. Norman, Oklahoma. Johnson, Vermont. Marietta, Georgia. A bunch from places in Virginia I'd never been — Sandston and Ashland and Blackstone. Their horses were gorgeous, mostly bays and chestnuts, but also dapple grays and a couple of enormous white Warmbloods. Sonny was one of the only ones with bright white socks.

Wayne didn't say much. I figured he was as blown away

by the horses and riders as I was. There was nothing to talk about, really. Usually at a show, some kids are great, some are terrible, some are having a good day, and some bad. You see a horse try to kick another one, or a rider who can't make a horse go at all. But here, everyone was great, and all these horses looked as if they cost a million dollars. When I glanced over at Wayne, he was just looking straight ahead, chewing.

I saw the steam rising off a hot horse's back, and it reminded me of the white cows at home, steaming as they stood out in the rain. I wondered if I'd gotten to be any more like those cows, the way they ignored the rain pouring down on them. I didn't think I would ever be able to ignore it, but I was starting to get used to it.

We'd all have to work on the flat after this. Then those who made the cut would be tested again. The test could be anything. Sometimes they made riders switch horses. I wanted that to happen. I wanted Kelly to get some hot horse she didn't know how to ride, and I wanted to ride one of those beautiful white Warmbloods.

Kelly was finishing her round. She looked pretty good, and I congratulated her when she finished. Her eyes opened wide, and she said, "Thanks," like she was surprised I'd said something nice to her. That made me feel kind of terrible and kind of good at the same time.

When the last riders were going, I went back to get Sonny ready for the flat class, and I brought him out.

Wayne gave me a leg up, and I looked into the stands as I gathered the reins.

Melinda was watching from the third row. She saw me and waved. I couldn't believe it. She was wearing her nice purple sweater and her hair was done. I waved back and pointed her out to Wayne.

"I know," he said. "She told me she was thinking about it, but not to say anything in case she couldn't come."

"How'd she get up here?"

"Train from Clifton Forge. You know what's right below Madison Square Garden?"

"What?"

"The train station."

I laughed. I couldn't imagine her getting on a train all by herself, but I was so glad. I loved the thought of her sitting alone and reading a magazine, taking a nap, doing whatever she wanted.

"Did she see my round?"

"She did. Now, forget about her and focus on what you're doing, Sidney. She'll be here when you're done."

Riders filed into the ring and started to trot. We were going thirty-five at a time. Riders were trying to get the judges' attention, trying to stand out. The trick was to circle right in front of them but to look as if you had no other choice.

Everybody was doing that at once, and it was a mess. I watched several groups go, then it was my turn. When I got into the ring, I stayed at the rail.

"Riders, hand gallop, please," the announcer called. Thirty-five horses, galloping in a circle, everyone trying to stand out. I nearly collided with another horse.

"And . . . halt . . ."

I sat up and pulled Sonny to a dead stop. For some reason he trotted a few steps first, an honest mistake but one that could keep me from making the cut.

"Counter-canter . . ."

We had to make our horses canter on the opposite lead. If they were going clockwise, we had to make them canter on the left lead. This required great balance, and the horse had to be attentive to your legs. The worst thing you could do was to get the wrong lead, then pull back to a trot and correct it, like I saw another rider do. I dug in my inside heel, planted my right hand into his neck, and shifted my weight to the outside, just a little. Sonny got it.

We did a few more gaits, cantering without stirrups, then a sitting trot. Then, suddenly, Sonny stumbled hard. I almost came off. I figured he'd gotten distracted by all the excitement.

The announcer called for us to line up in the center of the ring. This was the moment when I'd find out if we'd made the cut.

"Those riders whose numbers are called, please form a new line."

They called five numbers, then ten, then Kelly's. She smiled, and I heard Dee Dee cheering.

Then I heard my number.

I pushed Sonny forward to line up with the others, but he wouldn't move. I gave him some leg, and I felt him lurch forward in a sickening, unnatural way.

He wouldn't put weight on his front leg. He was lame.

I jumped off to see if something was caught in his foot. Nothing there. Wayne rushed into the ring to help me. He picked up Sonny's hoof and checked once more.

"He's got pain up high. It's not his hoof," he said.

I saw Dee Dee turn to Martha and smile.

I heard someone on the rail say, "He's lame. She's out."

I pulled Sonny out of the ring by the reins, watching him limp. I heard some people gasp. Wes came over and felt Sonny's legs — nothing. I felt them, too — nothing wrong. Then Wes pressed on Sonny's shoulder, and the horse jerked away.

"He pulled a muscle. Bad," Wes said.

"We can soak it. We can walk him . . . Maybe he's got a cramp," I said.

"Sid, you can't ride him." Wes couldn't even look at me when he said this.

Wayne felt Sonny's shoulder, Sonny pulled back, and Wayne just looked off at the crowd.

I couldn't look at any of them. I couldn't look up into the stands at my mother. I told Wayne to tell her not to come down. I dreaded hearing everyone say, "You did great—it wasn't your fault," over and over. I didn't want to hear how close I'd come. If it had happened to Kelly, or most of these other riders, they'd have a backup horse. But not me. Maybe someone would lend me a horse. I couldn't bear the idea of asking Dutch and having him refuse. I thought about asking the girls from the stall next to mine, Caroline and Laura, but there was no time—I didn't even know where they were. Martha sat near the rail, reading her program, and didn't look at me.

I felt far away from everyone and utterly alone, with no safety net.

We walked Sonny to his stall slowly, put him inside, and gave him some hay. Poor horse—he'd done such a great job for me, and now he was in pain. I gave him bute and rubbed liniment onto his shoulder.

Then Wayne pointed at Sub.

"Ride him."

"Screw you," I said.

Wayne dug through my tack trunk, pulled out the electric clippers, and plugged them in.

"It's not funny," I said.

Wayne started clipping Sub's face.

Wes came over and saw what Wayne was doing. "Holy cow!" he said.

"No way," I said.

"How long would it take to braid this horse?" Wayne asked Wes.

"Twenty minutes. Won't be the best job, though."

"Do it." Wayne was clipping Sub's legs.

"He needs shoes," said Wes.

"I'm not riding Sub."

"I just trimmed him the other day," said Wayne.

"Wayne, he needs shoes!" said Wes.

"Well, he don't have them," said Wayne.

Wes pulled Sub out into the aisle and tied him up next to the stall. He jogged away and came back with the farrier, who took a look at Sub's feet and then brought over his tools.

"Just tack 'em on," said Wayne.

"Why don't *you* ride him," I said to Wayne. "You can break *your* neck."

They ignored me. Wes hopped up on the stool and was braiding like a fiend while the farrier worked. Sub could not have cared less. He leaned all his weight onto the farrier, who had one of Sub's hooves between his knees, trimming the edges. The farrier shoved him over and cursed.

"His mane is nice and dirty," Wes said.

It was nice watching this, because they cared, but it was sad, because it would never work.

The fuzz in Sub's ears came off and floated to the ground, then the shaggy hair under his chin. Wayne clipped the hair along the back of Sub's legs and around his feet. I had to admit, Sub was starting to look respectable.

Wayne put Sonny's bridle onto Sub and adjusted the buckles on the side. "Still got a head the size of a moose."

He put my saddle onto Sub's back, the girth strap barely fitting around his big belly. "Still got a belly the size of a hippo," Wayne said.

Then he grabbed a rub rag and wiped Sub down, still talking to him. "But you know, Submarine?" he said. "It ain't about your big head or your fat belly. It's about finding out who the best rider is. Even if she is on a fat old pinto that her father bought in Dunn's Gap from a crooked horse trader"—Wayne turned to face me—"for *her*."

"Shut up," I said.

"He bought this horse for you."

"He bought Sub for himself," I said.

"He bought him for you. That man knew how to pick a horse like no one I ever met. Lot better than I ever did. He picked out Sub for you, as a colt. He loved this horse."

I felt my throat tighten and tried to hold it in, but I let out a sob.

"He loved his color. Sub's a skewbald pinto, brown and white, Jimmy's favorite. And he's got these strong legs and big tough feet, and a heart the size of a watermelon. Jimmy could see that. When Jimmy found him, he was sharing an old run-in shed with a mama pig and her babies."

Tears were rolling down my cheeks now, but I couldn't move a muscle to wipe them away.

"You know why we were at that man's house, where we found Sub?"

"You were running moonshine," I said.

"No ma'am. That was just the story we told so nobody would know we were horse-shopping for a little girl. We had a reputation to protect. Jimmy looked high and low for a horse for you."

"He did?"

"We looked at every goddamn horse for sale in Virginia and North Carolina. And this is the one we found. Right there in Dunn's Gap."

I cried harder, looking at Sub, him looking back at me. I touched his big white cheek, and he closed his eyes.

"You a catch rider yet?" asked Wayne.

I buried my face in Sub's neck and cried.

"Stop it. You got a job to do," Wayne said.

I remembered how I used to gallop Sub along the hay field, knowing he loved it. He would jump anything. When I was on Sub, we were partners. Just now, I had been worrying about how he would look, what other riders would think, and not remembering how much fun he was to ride, how much he loved being ridden.

We waited a few minutes for Wes to finish braiding. Then I took the reins and led Sub out of the stall. I tightened his girth and got on.

"Fat as a pig. I can't even see my feet," I said. I looked down at his braids.

Wayne grabbed Sub's bridle and looked him in the eye. "You take care of her," he said.

I took Sub into the warm-up ring and picked up a trot. People were watching us. With his brown and white markings, Sub didn't look like any other horse at the show. He wasn't fine-tuned or sensitive, but he was athletic and honest.

If only he hadn't been standing out in a field eating for the past three years . . .

A couple of people looked at him and grinned. "Who rides a pinto?" I heard a trainer say.

"The American Indians did," Wayne said loudly, so I could hear. "They used 'em as warhorses. I wouldn't want to compete against a warhorse, myself."

Sub was looking around. He wasn't sure what was going on, but he wasn't spooked. I couldn't think of the last time he'd worn a saddle. We jumped back and forth over a vertical, and Wayne raised it up higher. Sub didn't blink at it. It was just like we were at home.

Wayne waved me over to the in-gate, where he stood with Wes. Dutch and Dee Dee were nearby, talking to Kelly, who was on Idle Dice.

"They might ask you to switch horses," Dutch said to Dee Dee.

"We'll scratch before we switch horses. No one is riding this horse but Kelly."

I wondered if that was true or if Kelly would put Idle Dice's name into a hat for some other kid to draw.

"They're holding the class for you. I told them we changed mounts. Go look at the new course," Wes said to me.

"What is it?" I asked.

"Ten fences, no stirrups," Wayne said.

I thought about riding Sub in Madison Square Garden over fences that were three feet six inches, without stirrups, and I just laughed. I hoped I could stay on.

In the ring, the jump crew was setting up a huge wall. It looked four feet tall from where I stood. "That's not three foot six," I said, taking my feet out and crossing the stirrups over Sub's withers.

"Listen, if that horse wants to, he can drag his fat ass over it. Simple as that," Wayne said.

They announced the order. There were twenty of us. Kelly was first, I was last.

Kelly had a tough ride ahead of her. But that horse was on autopilot and she knew she'd make it, so she could relax — be a passenger and pose. She added a stride down one line, and it didn't look great. And she did hang on for dear life going over that wall. I sighed with relief when it was over.

The next horse refused a jump and was eliminated. Except for a few pulled rails and some bad equitation over the bigger fences because the riders didn't have stirrups, the rest of the class did fine.

Finally, it was our turn. Win or lose, good or bad, this could be the last round of the show. My hands were sweating, and I wiped them on my coat. I looked up at Mama.

"On course is number seventy-two, Sidney Criser from Covington, Virginia."

I was going to ride boldly. I was going to win it or blow it, but I was going for it.

We walked into the ring, and Sub's ears perked up as he looked at the first fence. He jumped big, and I grabbed a handful of braids in order to hang on. We dug deep into the turns, and I felt him drop his head and play with the bit just like he used to when we were out in the field. Another fence, another oxer, the fan jump not perfect but fine, and I was still on. Finally, it was time for the wall. The last jump. It looked huge.

"Come on, Sub," I said. I dug in my heels and pointed him at the jump. He locked his eyes on it, gathered his haunches up under him, and left the ground. I hung on for dear life.

When he landed, I slowed him down to a trot and we left the ring. My mind was blank, and then it all started pouring in. I reached down to pat Sub's neck and saw that I had pulled out two of his braids.

Wayne laughed: "Ha!" He grinned and patted Sub hard behind the saddle. Mama came down from the stands and congratulated us.

After a couple of minutes, they called ten of us to ride back into the ring. Just ten, including Kelly and me. I didn't know if there were more tests or if this was it. We lined up, not looking at each other. I was nervous as hell. I had been thinking so much about the next steps, and now there was nothing to do but wait. The other riders looked anxious and excited.

The judge and another official walked in with a huge silver plate and a box of ribbons. This was it.

"Tenth place goes to number three hundred twenty-two . . ."

I was going to place.

He called ninth, then eighth. I kept counting to make sure there were ten of us in the ring.

"Third place goes to number twenty-nine, Kelly Wakefield."

I beat Kelly.

"And reserve champion of this year's ASPCA Maclay Finals goes to number seventy-two, Sidney Criser of Covington, Virginia."

My face got hot as a poker, and I thought I might pass out. I was reserve champion — second place!

The judge brought me a beautiful silver plate, smaller than the one I'd seen but gleaming like a mirror. She handed me a tricolor reserve ribbon in red, yellow, and white and a navy horse blanket. She smiled so hard when she handed them to me that I wondered if she thought I was someone else.

"And the 2012 ASPCA Maclay Championship goes to number one hundred nineteen, Jane McFarlane from Marietta, Georgia!"

It was a girl I had seen go late in the order, an elegant rider with a long-legged Thoroughbred.

"Good job," she said.

"You too," I said.

I posed with Sub for an official photo, and then I dismounted and they took another one with Sub's head over my shoulder, the ribbon hanging from his bridle, the silver plate in my hand.

"I love you," I whispered to Sub.

He rested his head on my shoulder and closed his eyes.

When Dutch came over and shook Wayne's hand, my heart almost burst. I hugged Wayne, then Mama. None of us said a word. I was all choked up and figured they were, too.

"Gee, I'm glad you didn't sell him to Chew-Gum for a thousand dollars," I said when I could speak.

Wayne laughed. He and Mama walked back to the stalls while people came over and congratulated me and asked about Sub.

Finally, I took Sub back to the stalls, my arms and legs feeling light, everything feeling easy. Wes was moving in the same direction in front of me. When he turned around and saw me, a warm smile spread across his face. He walked toward me and took my helmet and gloves to free up my hands. He brushed a piece of hair from my face, and then he wrapped his arms around me and held me tight. I thought I would die. I didn't want him to ever let go.

He took Sub's reins from me and walked him to his stall, took off his tack, and rubbed his head. Sub stuck his nose into a bucket of water and slurped half of it down without stopping.

I laughed. "Poor thing — he hasn't worked that hard in ten years!"

"You single-handedly brought back the pinto!" Wes said. "Cherokee would like to thank you from the bottom of his heart for making him cool again."

"Maybe we can take them out together sometime," I said.

Wes's smile faded. "I don't know if I'm going to be at Oak Hill for much longer. It's not the right place for me."

"Oh."

"But if I leave, I'll have to ask Cherokee to come with me," Wes said, smiling.

"Thanks," I said.

"For what?" he asked.

"You made me feel like I wasn't alone."

He leaned over and kissed me for real, his hand in my hair. I could feel the muscles in his back through his soft, worn T-shirt. I thought about how great he smelled, and then I almost laughed when I realized it was hoof polish.

"I have to finish up with the Oak Hill horses," he said, and he hugged me again and walked out of the stall. "I'll see you at home?"

"You riding back with Kelly?" I asked.

"No way. I'm in the truck with Edgar." Right then, I knew he and Kelly weren't together anymore. He had stuck with her to get her through the finals because he was a gentleman.

"Come over this week," I said. "We've got some horses that need work."

Caroline congratulated me and let me switch her horse's stall with Sub's, so Sonny and Sub were right next to each other. They stuck their noses over the wall between them and sniffed each other. Caroline also gave me a handful of sugar cubes for Sub. I gave him a couple, which he sucked right out of my hand. I gave a couple to Sonny, too.

I took my collar off, removed my grandmother's stock pin, and wrapped it carefully in tissue. I put it into the tack trunk to keep it safe. Then I straightened out the necklace Ruthie had made for me.

When I went outside with Mama and Wayne, it was getting dark. I went into a candy store and bought a big chocolate bar with hazelnuts for June. I watched the saleslady carefully wrap it in orange tissue paper with a shiny brown ribbon.

We bought hot pretzels covered in salt at a steaming cart on the corner.

Snow was beginning to fall, slowly at first, then harder, swirling around us.

"First snow of the year," Wayne said, holding his hand out and catching some flakes. I held my hand out too.

A horse pulling a carriage with tourists clomped by in the snow.

"Poor old horse don't have no pasture to graze in," said Wayne.

"He's lucky. He could be living at your house," I said. Wayne and Mama both laughed—"Ha!"—and we continued down the snowy sidewalk.

We found a bench and sat down together, Wayne between Mama and me. Mama had tears in her eyes, and they started to roll down her cheeks. It tore me up inside to see her cry, but somehow this was different. I knew she was thinking about Jimmy, and I also knew it was the happiest she'd been in a long time. She had made it here. We were in New York City together.

Wayne looked tired but happy. I knew I wouldn't be there if it weren't for him believing in me. He wanted to see me succeed because he knew me and he loved me. And I loved him back.

I knew I was a catch rider now. It ran in the family. I could ride anything, anywhere. People in the horse world knew this, but most important, I knew it. Now I could hang out by the rail at a big show in case someone needed a catch ride.

I watched cars quietly coasting through the snow, people holding out their hands, catching flakes and smiling, and I felt as light as air.

ACKNOWLEDGMENTS

THANK YOU, Adam, for everything.

I'm deeply indebted to Virginia horsemen Dale Stewart and Wayne Hooker for sharing their knowledge with me and letting me make the rest up.

Thanks to Sandi Hooper Melnyk, Jesse Thompson, Chester Cleek, Pete Criser, Mary Lynn Riner, Brian LaFountain, and all the people I met in Hot Springs, Virginia.

To my agent, Alice Martell, for taking a chance on me, and for being the best agent and friend a new writer could hope for. I lucked out when I met you.

Enormous thanks to my editor, Dinah Stevenson, for believing in my voice and for helping me believe in it too.

To Margo Meyer, Chandler Burr, Jane Hodges, Meg and Kristian Roebling, the Attanasios, Kathleen O'Donnell, Marc Kompaneyets, Claudine O'Rourke, Kit Pongetti, and Mark Stegemann.

To my teachers Howard Pugh and Dale Bishop.

To Maribel, Jaime, Ashley, and Jimmy Zavala, and to Angelica Cotrina.

To Marcus, Denise, Vinny, and Isabella Di Lucia.

To Philip Hirsh for his authentic and hilarious book about Bath County, *Voices from the Hollow.*

To Mitch Gordon.

I wrote much of this story in Indian Road Café, a sanctuary at the top of the island of Manhattan—thank you, Jason Minter, for creating it.

To Vermont Studio Center.

To Darren Johnson and Elizabeth Riley.

To Kaitlan and Carol Parker for letting me watch your journey to the Maclay Finals.

To Sandy and Joel Watstein for the long hours of babysitting.

Thank you to old Submarine and all the other horses I've met, especially the mean ones.